D0406013

Geronimo Stilton

Thea Stilton
THE SECRET OF
THE FAIRIES

Scholastic Inc.

Library of Congress Cataloging-in-Publication Data Available

ISBN 978-0-545-55624-8

Published by Scholastic Inc., 557 Broadway, New York, NY 10012.
SCHOLASTIC and associated logos are trademarks and/or registered trademarks of Scholastic Inc.

Stilton is the name of a famous English cheese. It is a registered trademark of the Stilton Cheese Makers' Association. For more information, go to www.stiltoncheese.com.

Text by Thea Stilton
Original title *Il segreto della Fate del Lago*
Cover by Danilo Barozzi and Flavio Ferron
Illustrations by Giuseppe Facciotto and Barbara Pellizzari
Color by Alessandro Muscillo
Graphics by Marta Lorini

Special thanks to Tracey West
Translated by Emily Clement
Interior design by Kay Petronio

12 11 10 9 8 7   16 17 18/0

Printed in Malaysia   108

First printing, September 2013

THEA STILTON AND THE THEA SISTERS

THEA · PAULINA · Colette

Violet · nicky · PAMELA

THE LAND OF ERIN

The Land of Erin is a fantasy land where magical creatures live. They are similar to creatures from the fairy tales of Ireland and other nearby lands. Some of their names and abilities, however, are unique to this strange world.

POOKAS: These mischievous creatures can change form. They most often appear as a black horse with shining eyes.

LAKE FAIRIES: They protect the secrets of Erin. They speak only in riddles, and if you can't answer, they will freeze you for a year!

GOBLINS: Always causing trouble, goblins have long noses and pointy ears. They live in the Canyon of Sounds, and they don't like intruders.

GREEN PIXIES: They live on the banks of the river in the Canyon of Sounds. They try to be helpful but sometimes get mixed up.

THE YUM FAIRIES: They are excellent cooks, but think twice before sitting down at their table. Fairy food comes at a price.

LEPRECHAUNS: These fairies are shoemakers, famous for their skills. When they aren't working, though, they like to play tricks.

GNOMES: These kind fairies live in the Enchanted Forest. They are small, with pointy hats and shoes.

BANSHEES: These fairies are very beautiful but always sad. They live alone, and you can find them by following their cries.

GUARDIANS OF TREASURE: These greedy goblins will do anything to get treasure. They live in the Gray Marshes.

RED CAPS: These creatures are the bullies of the fairy world. They are part of the Court of the Discontented.

STUDY, STUDY, STUDY!

At Mouseford Academy, the most difficult time of the year had arrived: exam time! The **THEA SISTERS** were busy studying for their Economics and Statistics class.

Nicky closed the book in front of her. "I can't keep my **EYES** open any longer!"

So tired!

"Tell me about it." **Violet** yawned.

"I'm going to bed. You can't **succeed** without sleep," *Colette* added.

"Or cheese," PAm said. "I need a sandwich."

Violet sighed. "I need a little more time. I just don't feel *confident*," she confessed.

Nicky patted her on the shoulder. "You'll be fine, you'll see."

PAULINA was busy scribbling **numbers** in her notebook.

"Don't you want a break?" Colette asked.

"I have to study this formula," she replied.

Her friends said good-bye and left the library.

Paulina buried her nose in her book. When she looked up again, she saw the rising SUN through the window. How long have I been studying? she wondered.

She walked to the window to feel the crisp breeze on her face. When she looked down, she saw . . . me, THEA STILTON! I was getting ready to teach a class on UNDERSEA INVESTIGATION techniques.

Oh, let me introduce myself! I'm a **SPECIAL** correspondent for my brother's newspaper, *The Rodent's Gazette*, and I sometimes teach at **MOUSEFORD ACADEMY**.

It's already dawn!

I was just returning from a dive, so I was still wearing my **wet suit**. My mask and flippers **DEFINITELY** looked out of place in the garden!

Curious, Paulina joined me outside.

"Good morning, Thea!" she said, smiling.

"Good morning, Paulina," I replied. "You're up **early** today."

Paulina yawned. "Actually, I haven't slept at all."

I noticed the **BOOKS** she was carrying under her arm. "Studying for exams?" I asked.

"Exactly. And Professor Datamouse is very demanding!" she said.

I smiled. "Cheer up! I have a fantastic surprise for the next semester."

Paulina's eyes sparkled with excitement. "Really? What is it?"

"I'm going to be teaching a special class on investigation under the sea," I revealed. "I spent some time inspecting the ocean floor around the island. There is evidence that these WATERS might have held a very interesting past."

"Can we all take the class with you?" Paulina asked. "Will we be able to dive and discover these MYSTERIES for ourselves?"

"Of course!" I replied.

"This is FABUMOUSE news!" she

exclaimed. "I'm going to tell the others."

As I watched her **RUN** out of the garden, I thought about how **LUCKY** I was. The Thea Sisters were such enthusiastic students! I'm always happy to spend time with them.

I had a meeting soon with Octavius de Mousus, the headmaster of Mouseford Academy, so I headed to my room for a shower. As I opened the door, I saw that someone had slipped a **Letter** underneath it. Who could have sent it?

A REQUEST
FOR HELP

I picked up the envelope and stared at it, speechless: It was from the **Institute of Incredible Stories** (I.I.S.).*

On the corner of the envelope, I saw the symbol for the **SEVEN ROSES UNIT**, one of the most secret departments in the I.I.S. Recently, I took a special **test** to see if I could join the department — and passed it! But I had just started my training. This was the first time they had contacted me.

I **QUICKLY** opened the envelope and began to read. . . .

CONFIDENTIAL!

* To learn more about the I.I.S., go to page 10.

I.I.S.

Dear Thea,

The Seven Roses Unit needs your help!
Nina, one of our most promising agents,
recently began studying Irish legends.
Twenty days ago, she left for Ireland to
conduct research. We haven't heard from
her in a week. It's as if she has vanished!
I need you to help me find her. If you
accept, call me for details at the number
on the back of this paper. Nina's life could
be in danger!

Sincerely,

Will Mystery

SEVEN ROSES UNIT

Seven Roses Unit

I **immediately** dialed the number. "Will, this is Thea Stilton."

"Thea! I'm so glad you called," he replied.

"Well, I had to. Your letter sounded **VERY URGENT**," I said.

Will lowered his voice. "I know you have just begun your training," he said. "But this is an **EMERGENCY**, and I know you have exactly the skills we need to solve this problem."

"You can count on me!" I said confidently.

"What can I do?"

"I need you to go to Ireland to find **Nina**, the agent who has disappeared," Will explained.

"The last time we heard from Nina, she said she

I.I.S.
Institute of Incredible Stories

SUPER SECRET RESEARCH CENTER
The I.I.S. was founded by a group of scientists dedicated to the study of unsolved mysteries. It is led by Mr. Alpha.

INVISIBLE HEADQUARTERS
To keep their research secret, the I.I.S. headquarters is hidden in icy Antarctica. It can only be reached by traveling through an underground tunnel and then passing through a hologram of a tower made of ice.

THE SEVEN ROSES

The Seven Roses Unit is the most secret department of the I.I.S. It is dedicated to the study of lands found in myths and legends. It is directed by Will Mystery, an expert researcher.

THE THEA SISTERS AND THE I.I.S.

Thea Stilton and the Thea Sisters worked with the I.I.S. in their adventure *The Journey to Atlantis*. Since then, Thea has become an official agent of the Seven Roses Unit, thanks to her great investigative skills.

was on the brink of an IMPORTANT DISCOVERY," Will continued. "We know that she was exploring some ancient ruins on a ROCKY island near CORK. Since you are an investigative journalist, we're hoping that you can track her down."

"I'll do my best," I promised. "You said Nina VANISHED a week ago. Where was she last seen?"

"Northeast of Cork, in Dunmore East, a town along the Irish coast," Will replied. "An **I.I.S. AGENT** will be waiting for you at the Dogwalk Inn. I will give you an envelope with instructions for reaching your destination and recognizing your agent."

"I'll prepare to leave **immediately**," I promised. "I'll look for your envelope."

I flipped my phone shut and began to pack. What if Nina was in some kind of trouble? There was **NO TIME** to waste!

TOP SECRET mission

My ears perked up when I heard a **cough** outside my door. Was someone spying on me?

I opened the door and saw **RUBY FLASHYFUR** walking down the hall, talking on her phone. Ruby was a student at the academy. She loved to be the center of attention and to cause trouble for the **THEA SISTERS**. But she was basically harmless.

I closed the door and finished packing. Then I put on my Seven Roses **pendant**, which I had received when I became an agent. I was ready to go! But first I had to say good-bye to the Thea Sisters. I found them by a classroom, waiting to take their exam.

The mouselets were early, as usual. They're very responsible. When they saw me with my **bag** on my shoulder, they looked surprised.

"Thea!" they all exclaimed at once.

"**HELLO!**" I replied with a smile.

Hello!

"Where are you going?" Paulina asked.

"Unfortunately, I have to leave early," I replied. "I'm on a **TOP SECRET** mission for the **I.I.S.**"

The Thea Sisters started talking all at once.

"How **exciting**!"

"What's the mission?"

"We should go with you!"

"I must go alone," I said firmly. "The mission is for the **SEVEN ROSES UNIT**, a top secret department. Besides, you need to take your exams."

Suddenly, I smelled very **STRONG PERFUME**. I turned to see Ruby Flashyfur peeking around the doorway. How **sneaky**!

"Hi, Ruby," I said, and she jumped in **SURPRISE**. "Shouldn't you be preparing for your exams?"

Her face turned **red** with embarrassment.

Hmpf!

"I was just . . . I mean . . . um . . ."

I shook my head. "Ruby, when are you going to learn? It's not nice to stick your whiskers into other rodents' *business*."

Ruby turned around and left in a huff.

"Let's go into the Reading Room," Colette suggested. "It will be empty at this hour, and we can talk without **prying ears** listening to us."

We went to the Reading Room and closed the door.

"**WILL MYSTERY**, the director of the Seven Roses Unit, contacted me," I explained. "He asked me to find a missing agent named Nina. She vanished under **MYsterious** circumstances."

"But you can't go alone!" Paulina exclaimed.

"You might find yourself in **DANGER**," added Violet. The other Thea Sisters nodded in agreement.

"Don't **worry** about me," I assured them. "I can do this on my own."

I took a quick **LOOK** at my watch. "I'm sorry, but I really must run. **GOOD LUCK** on your exams!"

The girls waved good-bye as I rushed *I'm off!* outside and down to the dock. I had to take the first **BOAT** to the nearest airport.

I was ready for my adventure to begin!

IRELAND, HERE I COME!

When I **BOARDED** the plane, the flight attendant handed me a magazine.

I took it from her and opened it, and an envelope slipped out. It was from Will Mystery. It contained a **PHOTO** of Nina and directions to the place where I was to begin my search.

I stared at the photo. The **I.I.S.** was counting on me to find her. Was I up for the **CHALLENGE**? As the plane soared through the sky, I planned my strategy.

After a while, I looked out the window. I **GASPED** in surprise at the marvelous view below me. Green fields rolled toward a deep blue sea. . . .

IT WAS IRELAND!

"How gorgeous!" I exclaimed.

After we landed in Dublin, I rented a car* and began my journey to Dunmore East, the village where Nina was last seen. I carefully made my way along the narrow, twisting road. The curves took me along the cliffs by the sea. I kept an eye on the water as I drove; it looked like there might be a **storm**. The waves sent **high** plumes of water up onto the cliffs.

Finally, after a few hours, I reached Dunmore East. The **tiny village** was tucked in County Waterford, northeast of Cork.

The village was lovely: a **CHARMING** cluster of fisherman's cottages built on a bay near a small dock. When I got out of the car, an unexpected *GUST OF WIND*

---

* In Ireland, vehicles are driven on the left side of the road. To make it easier to drive, the steering wheel is on the right.

almost knocked me off balance.

There was no one around to ask for directions, but the town looked small enough. I **WALKED** down the road, looking for my destination.

The delicious smell of something baking hit my snout, and I followed the scent. Then I heard a strange squeaking noise. I

looked up to see a wooden sign moving in the wind, with the name of the place it marked painted in green: DOGWALK. I **had arrived!**

SHOWDOWN!

While I was busy solving mysteries in **IRELAND**, the Thea Sisters were facing the mystery of their Economics and Statistics exam.

Paulina checked her notebook one last time. "Are you **worried** about the exam?" she asked her friends.

"You bet!" Pam replied. She took some **cheese crackers** from her backpack and started to munch nervously.

Professor Datamouse opened the classroom door. "The exam is about to start."

"Just one second!" Colette exclaimed with alarm. "I forgot to put on my perfume! I can't face this exam without the proper fragrance."

She took her favorite perfume, **Mousey**

...Sighs, from her purse, and spritzed a few drops behind her ears.

"Okay, now we can go in," she exclaimed with satisfaction.

The friends *smiled* with amusement. There was nobody like Colette! Now they all felt a little less nervous.

They entered the classroom and found their desks. Professor Datamouse stood in front of the room, holding the TEST papers in his paws.

He passed out the tests. "Let's begin!" he announced.

The THEA SISTERS scanned their papers. There were twenty multiple-choice questions followed by **TEN** difficult-looking word problems. They suddenly felt nervous again.

The room was *quiet* as the mouselets got

focused. Pam's stomach grumbled; taking tests always made her hungry! Paulina **ANXIOUSLY** tapped her pencil on the desk. Colette took a deep breath, letting the scent of Mousey Sighs calm her nerves. Violet **twirled** the ends of her long hair, and Nicky **scribbled** furiously on her paper.

"**TIME'S UP!**" Professor Datamouse finally announced.

The students all put down their PenCiLS and handed in their papers.

"How do you think you did?" Nicky asked her **FRIENDS** once they were in the hall.

"I couldn't solve the last problem," Colette

said with a **frown**.

"If you answered the rest, then you should be okay," Violet pointed out.

Nicky grinned. "You know, now that we're finished with our last exam for the semester, we should **surprise** Thea," she suggested. "It sounds like she was given a **TOUGH** mission, and she could probably use our help."

The Thea Sisters looked at one another and smiled.

"**GREAT IDEA!**" Pam exclaimed.

"Let's call **WILL MYSTERY**," Paulina suggested. "He can help us find Thea."

The friends *ran off* to call Will. They were on their own **mission** now — to find me, Thea Stilton!

ON THE OPEN SEA!

Paulina dialed the secret **EMERGENCY** number of the I.I.S.

"Who's calling?" asked a flat voice on the other end.

"We're the Thea Sisters," Paulina said **BOLDLY**. "We need to contact Will Mystery."

"One moment, please . . ."

A moment later, a **new** voice got on the line.

"This is Will Mystery. It's a pleasure to talk to you, **THEA SISTERS**. Thea has told me so much about you!"

The Thea Sisters . . .

"**Hello, Will!**" the five friends chimed in.

"Thea told us about the mission you gave her," Paulina said. "We want to join her. Can you tell us where she is?"

Will hesitated. "This mission is as **delicate** as a cheese soufflé," he said after a beat. "But you succeeded so well on your last mission for the I.I.S. that I think it is time for you to join the **SEVEN ROSES UNIT**. You'll have to come to headquarters for a **TEST**."

Come to HQ!

"We're ready," Nicky said. "We just aced our exams."

Will chuckled. "You won't have to study for this test. It's a DNA* test."

"But the I.I.S. is in Antarctica!" Paulina cried. "It will take **DAYS** to get there."

"I can arrange a special trip for you," Will assured them. "Get to the dock right away. A

* DNA is the genetic code that is unique to every living thing.

speedboat called *Rose of the Seas* will be waiting for you."

The friends got ready **QUICKLY** (even Colette!) and headed to the dock, where they found an I.I.S. **agent** waiting on the speedboat for them. They climbed on board and the boat took off at top speed.

"The **rumble** of this motor is music to my ears!" Pam exclaimed happily.

But as soon as they reached the open sea, the speedboat **SLOWED** to a stop. The Thea Sisters scanned the waters, confused. There were no boats on the horizon, and only seagulls flew overhead. What was going on?

Then the sea began to **BUBBLE**, and

Pleased to meet you!

foam covered the waves. The top of a **submarine** crested the water, and a rodent popped out of the top.

"Pleased to meet you, mouselets! I'm **WILL MYSTERY**!"

THE SEVEN ROSES

The five mice climbed into the submarine. Will swiftly steered the boat to the **SECRET BASE** of the I.I.S. He stopped the submarine near a large rock and pressed a **button**, and the rock slid open to reveal the entrance to the **SEVEN ROSES UNIT**.

The submarine entered and stopped at a

dock. They climbed out and Will led them to a door made of armored steel. He took a CRYSTAL pendant in the shape of a ROSE* from around his neck and placed it on a metal plate next to the door.

"Will Mystery," he said, and the door slid open.

Will grinned. "Welcome to the Seven Roses Unit!" he announced.

The mouselets followed Will to a laboratory. First, he used a special instrument to examine the irises of their eyes. Next, he recorded their **pawprints** and took samples of their hair for DNA testing.

They watched curiously as Will entered the data into a computer connected to an unusual-looking machine. The machine whirred, then stopped. A window opened,

* The rose-shaped crystal pendant is the official pass for those who work in the Seven Roses Unit.

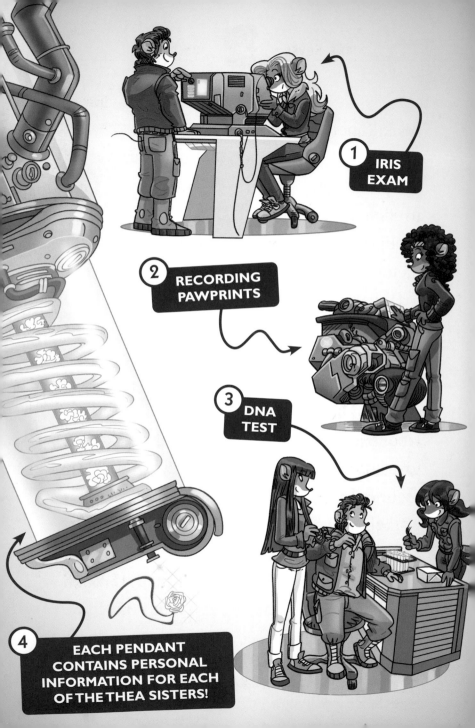

1 IRIS EXAM

2 RECORDING PAWPRINTS

3 DNA TEST

4 EACH PENDANT CONTAINS PERSONAL INFORMATION FOR EACH OF THE THEA SISTERS!

Here's your pendant, Paulina!

revealing five *crystal rose* pendants.

Will Mystery gave a pendant to each one of the Thea Sisters.

"Here are your official **passes**," he explained. "Don't lose them, and don't mix them up, because each pendant contains your personal information. When you use the pendant, you must say your **name**, because it is coded to the frequency of your voice. Your pass will give you access to all areas of the Seven Roses Unit, even the most **SECRET**."

Paulina looked at her pendant, fascinated. "It's beautiful. . . ."

Then a shrill sound rang through headquarters. *Beep Beep Beep! Beep Beep Beep! Beep Beep*

Beeep! Beep Beep Beeeeep! Beep Beep Beeeeep!

"That's unusual," Will said. He *ran* to the nearest computer, looked at the screen, and frowned.

"Oh, no!" he cried. He turned to the girls. "I'm sorry, but I must go. I need to tend to an **emergency**!"

"Can we help?" Paulina asked.

Will hesitated for a moment, but then he nodded. "**FOLLOW ME!** We need to go to the **Hall of the Seven Roses**!"

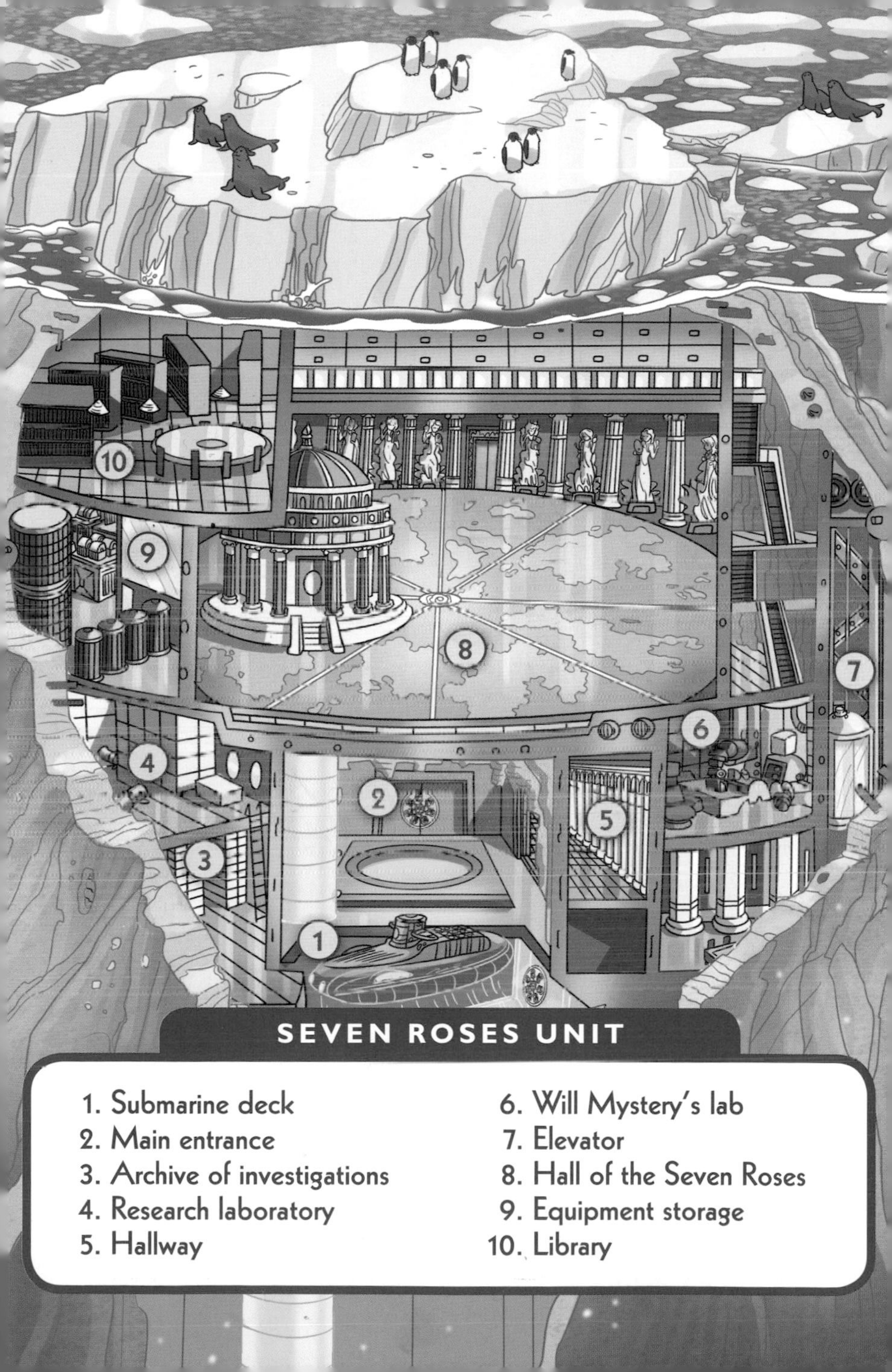

SEVEN ROSES UNIT

1. Submarine deck
2. Main entrance
3. Archive of investigations
4. Research laboratory
5. Hallway
6. Will Mystery's lab
7. Elevator
8. Hall of the Seven Roses
9. Equipment storage
10. Library

A WORLD IN DANGER

"I never dreamed I would need your **help** so soon!" Will said as they all *HURRIED* to the Hall of the Seven Roses.

"What happened?" Paulina asked.

"I'll know more when we get to the hall," Will replied. "But I may need you to accompany me on a very special **SECRET MISSION**."

"But then we won't be able to join Thea!" Violet exclaimed.

Will sighed. "I hope I'm wrong, but I think that THEA may be involved in this business."

When they came to the end of the hallway, at another STEEL door, Will stopped. "Do you promise to keep everything you see here a SECRET?"

The five friends nodded.

Satisfied, Will used his pendant to open the door. "You are about to enter the most secret room in our department, the **Hall of the Seven Roses!**"

The Thea Sisters passed through the doorway and gazed around in wonder at the beautiful space.

"This is a collection of the maps of all the **fantasy worlds** that we study here," Will explained.

"Fantasy worlds?" Paulina asked.

"Each real country has its own legends and stories," Will explained. "The **creatures** from these legends are real, and they live in **FANTASY WORLDS** that can be reached through special portals."

Speechless, the Thea Sisters stared at the maps on the floor and ceiling.

"Now one of these worlds is in **DANGER**," Will said. "The *Land of Erin*." He pointed to a map with a large crack in it.

"What does that mean?" Colette asked.

"These maps are **LIVING MAPS**, and they change when the land changes," Will explained.

Paulina's eyes widened. "So if there is a **crack** in the map . . ."

Will nodded. "Then

> **THE LAND OF ERIN**
> "Erin" is an ancient name for Ireland. The Seven Roses Unit uses this name to refer to the world in which creatures from legends from Ireland and surrounding areas live.

that means the Land of Erin is in great **danger**!"

"Hmm," Paulina said, thinking. "If I'm not mistaken, Erin is an **ancient** name for

Erin is Ireland!

Ireland. And this map looks just like Ireland. Are they the same place?"

"Nice observation," Will said. "The FANTASY WORLDS are all connected to places in the real world, where we live. Nina was studying IRISH LEGENDS, and she disappeared in Ireland, so I think there must be a connection between her disappearance and this **crack**." The friends fell into a worried silence.

"**Cheese** and **crackers**!" Pam finally exclaimed. "Since Thea went to Ireland, she could be in trouble, too. **WE'VE GOT TO DO SOMETHING!**"

"That's why I need you on this mission," Will said. "This is too **BIG** for one agent to handle — even a seasoned investigator like

Thea or Nina. We must go to the Land of Erin and **HELP** them!"

The friends **stared** at Will, confused.

"How can we get to the Land of Erin if it's a fantasy land?" Violet asked.

Will *smiled*. "Remember the portals I mentioned earlier? They are the key," he said. "You'll see what I mean very soon."

I need you!

STRANGE STORMS

While the Thea Sisters examined the **crack** in the map of the Land of Erin, I was investigating Nina's disappearance.

I stepped into the **Dogwalk Inn**. It was very dim inside. I looked all around for the I.I.S. agent, but everyone looked like a normal customer of the restaurant.

Following Will Mystery's instructions, I walked up to the bar and sat down next to a **freshly baked** cake. After a few moments, a **red-furred** rodent sat down next to me and ordered a hot chocolate.

"Is that a honey cake?" I asked him, pointing.

"No, that's an **OAT CAKE**, a typical Irish dessert," the rodent responded, without

raising his eyes from the counter.

Those were the CODE WORDS I had been instructed to hear! He was the I.I.S. agent!

"I'm Thea Stilton. Will Mystery sent me," I said.

"I know," he replied. "I'm Agent Ted O'Malley. Follow me."

We went outside, where a strong *gust of wind* hit us.

"Is it always this windy?" I asked, pulling my jacket tightly around me.

"No," Ted answered. "But a few weeks ago, we began to have strange STORMS and recorded **earthquakes** on the ocean floor. Nina told me that she thought they were a sign of KING WAVESHAKER'S anger."

"Waveshaker?" I asked.

"The king of the Land of Erin, the **mythical** world related to Ireland," Ted explained.

"Why is he so **anGRY**?" I asked, intrigued.

"That's what Nina was trying to find out," Ted replied. "The only thing I know for sure is that the *gusts of wind* are getting worse."

I thought about this. "So what can you tell me about Nina's disappearance?"

Ted slowly pushed back his hat, looking at me with intense **BLUe eyeS**. "The last time she was seen, she was headed for a rocky island with ancient ruins, just off the coast."

"Why would she go there?" I asked.

"She came to Ireland to **SEARCH** for a link to the Land of Erin," Ted replied. "Maybe she found it. That's what worries me. She should have **reported** her findings **IMMEDIATELY**. But we've heard nothing."

He took a map from his pocket. "If we want to find her, we need to take a **BOAT** to the island."

He gazed out toward the sea. "The waters are getting more **DANGEROUS** by the minute, so we'll have to tie up the boat tightly when we land. Otherwise we might never return . . . **Just Like Nina**."

I looked out at the rough waters, and a shiver ran down my spine. Would this be my last mission?

THE MYSTERIOUS CASTLE

Thirty minutes later, Agent O'Malley and I were racing across the **CHOPPY** waves on a speedboat bearing the symbol of the Seven Roses.

Don't worry!

"Will we make it in this *wind*?" I asked.

"Don't worry, I'm an expert **sailor**," Ted replied, hitting the gas.

Thoughts about Nina were TURNING OVER in my mind. "Do you know if Nina was alone when she headed for the ancient ruins?"

Ted nodded. "Unfortunately, yes. I offered

to accompany her, but she was very excited about something and in a great **HURRY**. She insisted on going by herself."

I didn't say anything, but Ted's words struck home. Nina and I shared the same fault — I often went off investigating on my own, and it had gotten me into **TROUBLE** many times. Now I had come to Ireland **without** the Thea Sisters. I imagined they were *relaxing* on a beach somewhere, glad to be done with their exams.

Lost in thought, I heard Ted say, "See that little cove? We'll dock there. The **ROCKS** will protect us from the wind."

I looked up to see that we had reached the island. After we docked, the boat rocked dangerously as Ted tied it up. Then we climbed onto the rocky shore, where we found the ruins of a crumbling stone **CASTLE**.

As we stepped through the wide front doors, a blast of **icy** air hit us.

The doors opened into an **ENORMOUSE** hall with a ceiling so high that it was difficult to see where it ended.

Ted shone his **FLASHLIGHT** around the room. "I don't see anything interesting," he said.

But I noticed something — a **HOLE** in the floor.

It's a castle!

"It looks like a **PASSAGEWAY**," I guessed.

Ted aimed the light at the hole and saw stairs that descended into the darkness.

"Should we go **DOWN**?" he asked.

"Of course!" I replied.

So we walked **DOWN**, **DOWN**, **DOWN**, until finally we saw a faint *LIGHT* at the bottom, and heard the sound of **WATER**.

We took the last step and found ourselves in a **CAVE** with the stormy sea just beyond the opening. Quickly, we began to search every corner for some sign of Nina.

"There's nothing here," Ted said, frowning. Then his eyes lit up. "**WAIT! LOOK HERE!**"

What's that?

Oh!

I followed the beam of the flashlight and found a **fur clip** shaped like a seashell on the cave floor.

"I **RECOGNIZE** that. It's Nina's!" Ted exclaimed.

"If Nina found this cave, she couldn't have left by the **sea** without a boat," he reasoned, his voice rising with excitement. "Maybe she found the **LINK** to the Land of Erin she was looking for! Maybe it's here in this cave."

"What kind of world is the Land of Erin?" I asked.

"It's a place where creatures from **myths** and **Legends** are real," Ted explained.

I started to feel excited, too. "You mean there could be a **PORTAL** to this fantasy world somewhere close by?"

Ted nodded. "It's possible. Let's keep looking."

I scanned the cave until I found a pile of **DRY BRANCHES** stacked up in the corner.

"They're juniper branches," I said. "But what would they be doing here?"

"Maybe Nina wanted to *LIGHT* up the cave so she could search for the portal," Ted guessed. He stacked up the WOOD in a pile, then took a box of matches from his pocket and lit the FIRE.

As the flames grew, I felt the ground tremble beneath my paws. To my amazement, the stone floor of the cave opened up, revealing another **STAIRWAY**!

"It must be the portal," Ted murmured in disbelief. "It really exists!"

It's the portal!

I knelt down and felt warm air WAFT UP to hit my face. In the distance, I could hear a mysterious melody. . . .

"We have to take the portal!" I said excitedly.

Ted shook his head. "You'll have to go alone. LOOK!"

He pointed to the wall of the cave, where the light from the fire **illuminated** some words we hadn't seen before.

Enter the portal if you dare.
Heed this warning and beware:
The flames of the fire must never die,
Or the portal will shut; this is no lie.

"That must be what happened to Nina," Ted said solemnly. "The fire went out, and she became TRAPPED there."

"Then I'm counting on you," I said, looking him squarely in the eye.

Ted nodded. "I will do my best to keep the **FIRE** lit. Be safe, Thea."

We shook paws and said nothing more. Then I took a deep *breath* and headed down into the **DARKNESS**. . . .

I'm counting on you!

An Amazing ELEVATOR!

I didn't know it at the time, but while I was **VENTURING** down the stone staircase, the Thea Sisters were entering the Land of Erin, too . . . by another route.

In the Hall of the Seven Roses, Will led the girls to a marble, domed structure carved with roses. He held up his pendant and said his name before the shining crystal door, and it opened immediately.

Will stepped in and motioned to the Thea Sisters. "Come inside! This is the **secret portal** that will take us to the Land of Erin."

They followed Will and found themselves inside an elevator made of clear CRYSTAL.

The door closed with a **whoosh**, and a

keyboard resembling the keys of a piano lit up on one of the walls. Will touched the keys, and a **MYSTERIOUS SOUND**, one the mouselets had never heard before, ECHOED around them.

The Thea Sisters tried to describe the

SOUND, but they couldn't. It seemed to be the tones of a **harp**, a **flute**, and a **violin**, all combined into one unique tone.

"Each fantasy world has its own special **FREQUENCY**," Will explained. "**Playing** the frequency on this keyboard allows us to travel to that world."

Violet **LOOKED** thoughtful. "So **MUSIC** is the bridge."

Will **nodded**. "Yes, that's right. But we must

be very careful. If we don't create the exact right **melody**, we could find ourselves in an **unknown**, dangerous land, and we might never be able to return."

The friends shivered and exchanged a nervous look.

Then the **MUSICAL** tones began to fade and were replaced by the **LILTING** sound of a woman's voice repeating one word:

Erin...Erin...Erin...
Erin...Erin...Erin...

IN THE LAND OF ERIN

The elevator *swirled* through a vortex of shimmering light and then came to a sudden stop. The doors opened onto a magnificent GREEN FIELD.

"Welcome to the Land of Erin!" Will cried.

"**Incredible!**" Paulina exclaimed, fascinated.

Welcome to the Land of Erin!

Colorful BUTTERFLIES danced over the green grass as it rippled in the gentle breeze. The sweet sound of songbirds filled the air. Above them, shades of purple and pink streaked the BLUE sky.

The Thea Sisters stared at the sight, enchanted.

"What a beautiful place," Nicky remarked, taking it all in.

"Where should we go?" Pam asked.

The Thea Sisters gazed around. The field seemed to extend in every direction, with nothing on the horizon.

It's not working!

Paulina suddenly had an idea. She took out her MousePhone.

"Let's try my navigation app," she said, but the phone just **buzzed** loudly and then shut off. She FROWNED. "It's not working!"

"So then, we're lost?" Colette asked nervously.

"Don't worry," Will said. "I brought a map with me from the Hall of the Seven Roses."

He produced the M A P from his bag and unrolled it in front of them.

"But how do you know our current location?" Violet asked.

Will looked up at the SKY. A flock of birds flew overhead.

"I suggest we go that way, toward the place those birds are coming from,"  he said, pointing at the distance.

"Why?" Paulina asked.

"Because right now it's early **morning**, and the birds are probably coming from an area with trees, where they spent the night," Will guessed.

Pam was perplexed. "And why are we looking for **TREES**?"

"Because we can climb to the top of one and look for a **REFERENCE POINT** that will tell us where we are on the map," Will explained. "Also, it's possible that an area of

1. Talking Stones
2. Valley of Wishes
3. Greedy Village
4. Green Forest
5. Cave of Sorrow
6. Gray Swamp
7. Enchanted Forest
8. Purple Mushrooms
9. The Door of Light
10. The Canyon of Sounds
11. The Emerald Lake
12. Forest of Leafy Trees

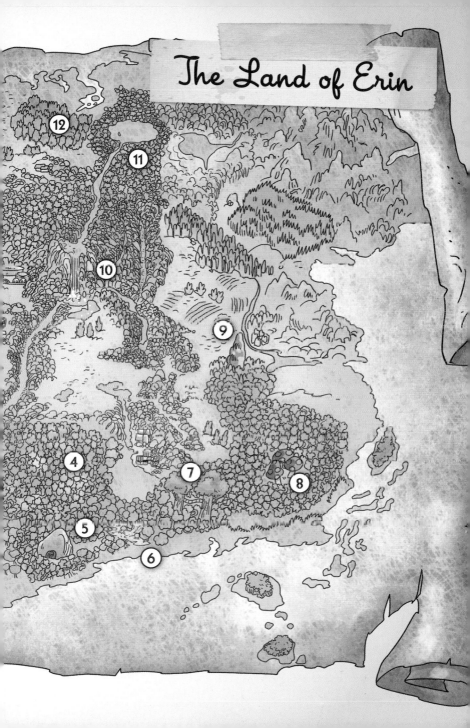

The Land of Erin

trees might be close to a **VILLAGE**, where we can ask for information."

Paulina looked at Will, impressed. She sometimes **DREAMED** about working at I.I.S. headquarters one day. She could learn a lot from a clever agent like Will Mystery. She **imagined** having her own office, filled with **BOOKS** about myths and legends

Someday . . .

from all over the world, as well as the latest **technology** and equipment. . . .

Nicky's bold voice got her out of her daydream. "Well, it's decided. Let's go look for some trees!"

A MISCHIEVOUS HORSE

The Thea Sisters and Will Mystery walked across the field until they reached the edge of a great **FOREST**. The tangled roots and branches of the tall trees formed a labyrinth along the forest floor.

Will **cautiously** led the group forward. Although he had studied the Land of Erin,

Be careful!

he had never visited before. He wasn't sure what to expect.

They soon entered a small clearing, where they noticed a large, **DARK** shape in the grass. Moving closer, they discovered a **HORSE** with a shiny black coat! The animal seemed to be fast asleep.

"It's beautiful," Colette whispered.

"It's strange that he hasn't noticed us," Violet observed.

"He's **SLEEPING**," Pam pointed out.

Will put a paw to his lips, and the friends **carefully** followed him past the sleeping horse. They made no sound as they trod on the soft grass, but the horse somehow sensed their presence. He opened his eyes and got to his feet.

"**Who goes there?**" he asked.

The horse had a strange, crackling

Of course I can talk!

voice, and his eyes shone with golden light.

"But . . . you can talk!" Nicky exclaimed in surprise.

The animal let out a great **yawn**. "Of course I can talk, my dear. Especially when someone disturbs my sleep."

Nicky still couldn't believe she was speaking to a horse. "We're sorry we woke you up."

"It happens often," the horse explained. "I am awake at night and sleep during the day. I am a **POOKA**."

"Is that a kind of fairy horse?" Paulina asked.

"I can take many forms," the pooka replied. "But, tell me, what are you doing here in the **Forest of Leafy Trees**?"

Will leaned toward the mouselets and

WHISPERED, "Be careful answering his questions. Not all creatures in these fantasy worlds can be trusted."

Then Will spoke up. "We're just here for a visit," he said casually.

Nicky couldn't take her eyes off the pooka. It would be amazing to ride him!

"Why don't you come for a *ride*?" the horse suggested, as if he had read her thoughts.

Nicky was speechless.

"*Be careful!*" Paulina warned.

Nicky jumped onto the pooka's back, and the horse immediately launched into a **GALLOP**. Even though Nicky was an expert rider, she could barely hold on.

"**Stop!**" she shouted.

But the pooka didn't even slow down. Was he trying to throw her off?

The horse **RACED** through the forest, narrowly missing the trees, and Will and the Thea Sisters chased after him.

"Please **slow down**!" Nicky pleaded. But the pooka kept going, and she held on as tightly as she could.

Then, without **warning**, the pooka stopped. Nicky lost her balance and **toppled** to the ground . . . landing in a puddle of **mud**. Angry, she looked up to see the pooka laughing.

Stop!

Naughty horse!

"There's nothing funny about it, you **NAUGHTY** horse!" she yelled.

Nicky tried to stand up, but she slipped in the mud.

The horse laughed again. "I must compliment you, my dear," he said. "No one has ever stayed on my back for so long."

Nicky pressed her paws into the mud, trying to steady herself. That's when she saw a green NOTEBOOK on the ground next to her. It must have fallen from the bag that the pooka wore around his neck.

"WHAT is this?" Nicky asked, picking it up.

"Oh . . . that . . ." the pooka

FALTERED, losing his cool. "I . . . I . . . took it from the Green Pixies. They live in the Canyon of Sounds, near the river."

"You mean you stole it?" Pam asked as she and the others arrived on the scene.

"Of course not!" the pooka said with a snort. "I was just playing a joke on the pixies. And, actually, it doesn't even belong to them. They couldn't read the strange symbols on the pages. They're the ones who **STOLE** it — from someone else."

He neighed and galloped away.

"He may look like a beautiful horse, but that pooka is very **rude**," Pam said, shaking her head.

Paulina, meanwhile, had opened the notebook.

"Is it a **diary**?" Colette asked, leaning over her friend's shoulder.

Paulina turned the pages, which were covered in faded **INK**. The writing on the page might have looked strange to the pixies, but Will and the Thea Sisters could read it just fine.

"It looks like a **travel** diary," Paulina remarked, turning to the first page.

"**'THE MYSTERIES OF ERIN,**'" Violet read. "Maybe there is something in here that will explain what is **THREATENING** this land!"

THE MYSTERIOUS CLUE

"Let me see," Will said, and Paulina handed the book to him. He **GASPED** with surprise. "This is Nina's diary!"

"I thought she disappeared in Ireland," Paulina said.

"Yes, but she was looking for a **portal** to Erin," Will explained. "She must have found it! This is her handwriting, for sure."

Paulina continued to **EXAMINE** the notebook. "Here's something. Nina wrote, 'King Waveshaker is **FURIOUS**. His anger is shaking the Land of Erin.'"

"That **EXPLAINS** a lot," Will said. "Waveshaker physically **shaking** the Land of Erin could be the reason for the **crack** that appeared on the map in the

Hall of the Seven Roses."

Paulina kept reading. "'The king will only be satisfied when what has been taken from him has been returned. Today, I discovered who is guilty of the theft. . . . '"

"Oh, no! The page is ripped!" Nicky exclaimed.

Colette frowned. "So, to save the Land of Erin, we have to return what was stolen from King Waveshaker. But we don't know what was stolen, or WHO took it!"

"But Nina knew," Violet pointed out. "Perhaps if we follow the trail she has recorded in this diary, we can find her."

Paulina nodded. "Good idea. Let's find those Green Pixies. They had the diary, so maybe they know where to find Nina."

"The pooka said that the Green Pixies live in the Canyon of Sounds, near the **river**," Violet remembered.

Will studied the map. "He also said that we're in the Forest of Leafy Trees. So then we must travel south, past the *Emerald Lake*."

Nicky climbed on top of a rock. "I think I can see a lake shimmering in the — **Whoa!**"

A terrible **rumble** shook the ground and

Nicky lost her balance once again, tumbling off the rock.

"Careful!" Colette cried out as Will rushed forward to catch Nicky.

"Thanks," Nicky said with a relieved sigh.

Paulina stared at the notebook. "I'll bet that was King Waveshaker. He must be very **ANGRY**. The Land of Erin really is in **danger**!"

I've got you!

THE LAKE FAIRIES

The Thea Sisters and Will Mystery walked through the forest.

"Let's hope that Waveshaker will *calm* down for a little while," Pam said.

Colette nodded. "I hope so. But we should **HURRY**, just in case. I have a feeling that we don't have much time."

Following Will's map, they made their way through the tangled forest as quickly as they could. For a time it seemed like the woods might not ever end, but they finally came to the edge.

The Emerald Lake lay before them, its blue-green water sparkling like precious **jewels**. They all stared for a moment, admiring its beauty.

"We're one step closer," Will murmured.

"We **MUST** find Nina, and learn what was stolen from King Waveshaker and who stole it."

We'll solve it!

"We'll **SOLVE** this mystery," Paulina encouraged him.

Will *smiled*. Paulina's optimism was contagious.

"Look, there's a **BOAT**!" Nicky cried, pointing to the lake. "We can get to the Canyon of Sounds more quickly if we row across."

"Good idea," Will agreed.

As they headed toward the **SHORE**, a feeling of peacefulness surrounded them. Then a gentle song filled the air, sweeter than anything they had ever heard.

"I'm not the only one hearing this, right?" Colette asked.

"Such a beautiful song . . ." Violet said. She began to walk toward the water.

"*Vi! Look out!*" Colette pulled Violet back just before she stepped into the water. It was as if she was in some kind of trance!

Colette was just in time. The surface of the water began to **ripple**, and to everyone's astonishment, three *beautiful* creatures emerged from the waves. The first had long, light hair the color of **WHEAT**. The second had a mane of shiny brown hair the color of the branches of a **tRee**. The third had gorgeous locks the color of **FIRE** crowning her face.

A SECRET . . .
OR A CLUE?

The three beautiful maidens wore flowers in their hair. Their faces shone with light reflecting off the surface of the lake. Their eyes, sparkling and serious, studied the Thea Sisters and Will Mystery.

"What gorgeous creatures!" Colette exclaimed admiringly.

"They may be beautiful, but can we **trust** them?" Nicky asked, remembering the trouble the pooka had caused.

"Maybe there is something about them in Nina's travel journal," Paulina suggested. She FLIPPED through the pages and then suddenly stopped. **"Here it is!"**

We must solve their riddles. . . .

She read out loud, "'There are **three fairies** who live in the Emerald Lake, and they guard secrets.'"

Will took the diary from her. "Nina's written that to cross the lake, you must solve the fairies' riddles. Then the fairies will tell you one of their PRECIOUS SECRETS."

Pam frowned. "Riddles? That sounds like some kind of TRICK. Maybe we should find another way to get to the Canyon of Sounds."

"I checked the Map. There's no other way," Will explained.

"Well, then let's get going," Colette said. She turned to the fairies and CaLLeD, "Hello! May we cross the lake?"

The Lake Fairies said nothing.

"Maybe they didn't understand," Nicky guessed.

"If you ask me, they understood just fine," Will said, noticing their **STERN** expressions.

Then the brown-haired fairy spoke up. "Now your feet shall not move from the GRASS. You must answer our riddles in order to PASS."

"What does that mean?" Pam asked.

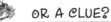

But the fairy's words quickly became clear when the Thea Sisters and Will tried to move. They were **STUCK** — as though their feet were nailed to the ground by some INVISIBLE FORCE!

"I can't move!" Paulina shouted.

"Me neither!" Nicky exclaimed.

"**WHAT DID YOU DO TO US?**" yelled Pam and Violet.

"You must first pay us **heed**, if you wish to proceed," sang the red-haired fairy.

"Only with **CUNNING** will you succeed," added the blonde fairy.

The brown-haired fairy finished the rhyme. "You may be kept here a **year** or more, if our riddles are something you ignore."

"We will answer your riddles," Will said boldly.

"Very well!" said the blonde fairy. "Here is the first riddle."

A gust of WIND rippled across the lake, and words appeared on the surface of the water:

They come to life in winter,
falling, falling, in the air.
But take care, for if you
touch them,
they will quickly disappear.

The Thea Sisters and Will concentrated, but Nicky spoke up first.

"The answer is **snow**!" she cried.

The Lake Fairies didn't respond. Nicky was **PUZZLED**. She was sure she was right. Then it hit her.

"Let me be more precise," she said. "The answer is **SNOWFLAKES**!"

"**CORRECT**," the blonde fairy admitted.

"Now for the second riddle," the brown-haired fairy announced.

Another *GUST* of wind blew, and new words appeared on the water:

It can run,
but never walks.
It has a mouth,
but never talks.
It never sleeps, but has a bed.
It wears no hat, but has a head.

Pam frowned. "This one seems more **difficult** to me."

"What has a mouth but can't talk?" Paulina wondered.

"It can run . . . has a mouth . . . and a bed," Colette mused. Then her eyes lit up. "I know! It's a **river**!"

"**CORRECT**," the brown-haired fairy said, sounding annoyed.

"Good job!" the other Thea Sisters exclaimed.

"Here is the third riddle," interrupted the red-haired fairy. Once again, the *WIND* wrote words on the water:

It's more precious than gold,
It can boil and bubble.
If you have too little or too much,
There will surely be trouble.

Will Mystery was the first to guess this one. "It's *water*!" he cried.

"CORRECT," the red-haired fairy sighed.

"Fantastic! Way to go, Will!" Paulina cheered.

"You've answered our questions three, and as promised, we'll set you **FREE**," the brown-haired fairy said. "You may cross the lake, with a **SECRET** to take."

The other fairies joined her, singing:

If the reason for a change is what you seek,
It's not in the air, nor under your feet,
Nor in the sea where you must start.
You must look in the depths of an unhappy heart!

After revealing their secret, the fairies disappeared into the Emerald Lake. **Circles** rippled over the surface, and then it once again became as smooth as glass.

"We can move!" Colette exclaimed, and the relieved friends happily hugged each other.

"The secret the fairies told us was very UNUSUAL," Paulina mused.

"It almost sounded like another riddle," Pam remarked. "Maybe it's some kind of **clue**."

"You mean a clue that will help us figure out what's WRONG with the Land of Erin?" Nicky asked, and Pam nodded.

"In any case, we're *free*!" Will said, untying the boat.

They all CLIMBED on board and Will took the oars. According to the map, they needed to cross the lake and then follow the *river* to the Canyon of Sounds. There, they hoped to find the Green Pixies who took Nina's notebook.

The journey across the lake was peaceful and calm. Fish swam in the **emerald** waters around them.

What an adventure!

"The fairies seemed a little **sad** when they went back into the lake, don't you think?" Paulina asked.

"Yes, I noticed that, too," Nicky responded.

"Could be," Colette said. "It must be very **DARK** at the bottom of that lake. That could get pretty depressing."

The Thea Sisters looked **DOWN** into the water.

"The fairies seemed quite unfriendly, but perhaps they were masking their **loneliness**," Violet suggested.

Pam nodded. "Maybe they were hoping we'd get stuck there so they could have some new **friends**."

"Those poor fairies," said Nicky. "We're so **LUCKY** that we have each other!"

PRISONERS!

After they crossed the Emerald Lake, Will Mystery steered the BOAT down the river. But the river waters were not as calm as the lake. The CURRENT became much stronger, and it became harder to steer.

"We're close to a WATERFALL!" Will exclaimed. "I need to dock the boat so that we can continue on foot."

He steered the boat to shore and pulled it onto DRY land. Everyone got out and began to walk along the riverbank. It wasn't long before they reached a bubbling, foaming **WATERFALL**.

The water cascaded down, shining with all the colors of the **rainbow**. It splashed down into a narrow canyon closed in by two tall rock walls on each side.

"It's the **Canyon of Sounds**!" Paulina exclaimed, pointing.

"The pooka told us that the Green Pixies live by the river," Violet remembered.

"Let's hope he was telling the TRUTH," Nicky grumbled. "Anyway, how are we supposed to get **DOWN** there?"

Pam walked to the edge of the canyon. "It looks like there's a **PATH** that goes all the way down," she reported.

"Then we must take it!" Will said. "There's no time to lose."

Careful!

Follow me!

Walking in **single file**, they carefully made their way down the path. It was **STEEP** in many places, but they all managed to keep their balance.

When they **FINALLY** reached the bottom of the canyon, Will walked over to the river and dipped his hand in the water.

"It's so beautiful and CLEAR," he said admiringly.

Then something pushed him from **BEHIND**! Will

looked up to see an army of small creatures descending on them.

The creatures had **LONG** noses and **POINTY** ears, and wore **GREEN** caps. They quickly tied up Will and the Thea Sisters.

"You are our prisoners!"

one of the creatures yelled.

in the eanyon of sounds

The Thea Sisters and Will struggled to get out of their ropes, but the creatures had tied them very **TIGHTLY**. To make matters worse, they looped the ropes through **STAKES** and then drove the stakes into the ground.

"Hey! Watch the fur-do!" Colette snapped at one of the creatures.

You're our prisoners!

"You'll pay for this, you **cheeseheads**!" Pam cried, giving the nearest creature a firm kick.

Paulina scanned the area, looking for some way to escape. But the situation seemed **hopeless**.

"Who are you?" Will asked as he struggled to get free.

"We are **goblins**," the creatures replied at the same time. "And this is our land!"

"Let us go!" Colette wailed.

Once again, the goblins all spoke together. "**YOU WANT OUR MINE**, and you'll never get it!"

"We don't know anything about a mine," Paulina protested. "We were just passing through."

"We don't believe you," the goblins said.

"It's the truth! We don't want to HARM you," Nicky told them.

The goblins formed a circle and then began to talk in HUSHED tones. When they returned, they seemed to be smiling in a friendly way.

"Do you think they'll let us go?" Colette whispered.

But before the goblins could speak again, a

sound like a thousand **BELLS** flowed through the canyon. The goblins looked **terrified**, and quickly ran away.

The Thea Sisters and Will didn't know why the goblins left, but they had a bad feeling. Anything that could frighten goblins must be pretty **SCARY**!

Soon a group of canoes appeared on the river, carrying **strange** passengers: tiny GReen creatures.

The first one to reach shore somersaulted out of the canoe, and the **BELL** he wore around his neck jangled.

"Nice work, I have to admit," he said, taking a **KNIFE** out of his jacket.

Colette tried to swat him away with her paw. "What are you doing with that?"

By now, the other creatures were on shore. They looked at each other and shrugged, confused.

"Let's get to work," the first one said, and he started to CUT the ropes that were binding the prisoners.

Working quickly, the little green men soon freed the Thea Sisters and Will Mystery.

"Thank you for your help. You SAVED us!" Will said as soon as he was back on his feet.

Let me help you.

Thanks! You were great!

Ha, ha, ha!

Hee, hee, hee!

Colette turned to the two creatures who had helped her. "Thank you! You set me free . . . without harming my outfit!"

"It was nothing," one of the creatures replied. "Those goblins are becoming worse and worse. They keep invading the territory of the Green Pixies."

"You're the Green Pixies?" Paulina asked.

"Of course! We live in this canyon, the Canyon of Sounds, along with the goblins. They live in the forest, while we live on the riverbanks. Today, the goblins invaded our territory to go fishing in the river, so we came to protect it . . . and found YOU!" another pixie explained.

"We're very happy that you found us," Paulina said. "Not just because you helped us, but because we were looking for you. We need information about this notebook."

She showed them Nina's travel diary.

"Ah, so you have it now?" the pixie asked. "It was a gift from the Yum Fairies in exchange for a sack of potatoes!"

"A sack of potatoes?" Violet asked.

"Yes, of course," the pixie replied. "We pixies grow the **BEST** potatoes. And since the Yum Fairies are excellent cooks, they are always looking for the finest ingredients for their delicious dishes."

"They're the best cooks in the whole Land of Erin!" another pixie piped up.

"Can you tell us where the Yum Fairies live?" Colette asked.

One of the pixies pointed toward the forest. "We can do more than that. We can take you to them!"

His companions looked at him, excited.

"You mean we can guide them?" one asked.

"What a **wonderful** plan!" another said.

"Then it's settled," said the pixie. "After all, who knows this land better than we do?"

"That's very KIND of you," Will said.

Will and the others didn't know it, but although the Green Pixies loved to GUIDE travelers, they were famouse for getting lost. They had no sense of direction!

"Let's get going!" the pixies cried merrily.

And they were on their WAY.

We'll take you to the Yum Fairies!

ARE WE LOST?

Hours later, the Green Pixies were still leading the Thea Sisters and Will Mystery through the forest.

"I think I've seen that rock before," Colette pointed out.

"And those three **TWISTED** plants," Nicky added.

The pixie leading the way paused. "Hmm. Maybe we should have taken a **left** at that boulder back there. Or maybe it was a **RiGHT**...."

? **? "Are you saying that we're lost?" ?**

Pam asked. "I thought you said you knew this land well!"

"Well, once in a while we get a little **confused**," the lead pixie admitted.

"Yes, especially when we're **HUNGRY**," said another pixie. "We probably shouldn't have traded all of our potatoes."

Are we lost?

"So I suppose it's possible that we're **very, very lost**," said the lead pixie.

The Thea Sisters were speechless.

"What do we do now?" Paulina wondered.

Will looked up at the **SKY** through the tree branches.

"I see **SMOKE**," he said, pointing.

The others followed his gaze.

"Maybe there's a village over there," Violet guessed.

"Or a house," Nicky suggested.

"Let's follow the smoke and see where it

LEADS us," Paulina said. "Maybe we'll find someone who can tell us where the **Yum Fairies** live."

"**Great idea!**" Will exclaimed, smiling at her.

The pixies seemed to be relieved that they were no longer leading the way. They whistled and jingled their bells as they walked. The happy tune was interrupted only by their **grumbling** stomachs.

"Oh, we're looking for a TREAT, for something very nice to EAT," they sang.

Paulina smiled at the pixies. So far, she and her friends had met several strange and amazing creatures in this land.

Will noticed her smile. "What are you thinking?" he asked.

"I'm just amazed by this place," she said. "It would be a shame if it were to disappear

We'll do it!

forever. I hope we can figure out what's wrong."

"Don't worry," Will said. "We'll find Nina and figure out why King Waveshaker is **ANGRY**. We've already found some great clues."

Paulina nodded. She admired the agent's ability to stay **CALM**, no matter what the situation.

They walked in the direction of the smoke until they came to some short, stubby trees laden with strange **red fruit**.

"Are those palm trees?" Colette asked. "How odd!"

"This is a **warm** climate, suitable for palm trees," Violet observed. "Although I have never seen **red** fruit growing on palm trees before."

"Don't forget, nature works differently in fantasy worlds," Will reminded them.

"**Cheese and crackers!** Look over there!" Pam suddenly exclaimed, pointing past the palm trees.

There, in the middle of a clearing, was a truly **amazing** sight.

HOW DELICIOUS!

"It's a BANQUET!" Pam said, her eyes wide with surprise.

"Why is there a dining table in the middle of the forest?" Nicky wondered.

"It's **beautiful**," Colette said admiringly.

The table was set with GLEAMING candlesticks, **GLASS** goblets, and shining silverware.

"Could this be the home of the Yum Fairies?" Paulina asked, turning to the pixies. But they were gone!

"Did they get lost again?" Colette asked.

Nicky frowned. "It's like they VANISHED. Which is a shame, especially since they were so hungry, and this place is set for a feast!"

"I hope they're not in TROUBLE," Violet said.

"Me, too," Colette said. "They may be terrible guides, but they are very nice."

Will looked up at the sky. "We should find out if the Yum Fairies live here before it gets dark," he said.

The mouselets nodded, and they made their way toward the little cottages that circled the clearing.

The sound of a rumbling stomach interrupted the silence.

"Is that the Green Pixies?" Paulina asked.

Pam grinned. "No, it's me," she admitted. "Seeing that table made me realize how

hungry I am. We haven't eaten in hours!"

Her *friends* all suddenly felt hungry as well.

"Now I know how the Green Pixies felt," Colette said sympathetically.

The clearing was deserted, but smoke poured from the **chimneys** of all three houses.

"Someone must be home," Pam guessed.

"Let's **knock**!" Nicky said, walking up to the first cottage.

Colette touched her paw to one of the smooth walls. "How interesting. This house is made of clay."

Violet pointed to the flowers and leaves that adorned the windows. "The **DECORATIONS** are beautiful. Whoever lives here must be an artist."

Pam walked up to another cottage. "This one is pretty, too. And what a great smell,"

she said, sniffing the air.

TANTALIZING SCENTS floated past their noses: bread fresh from the oven, gooey melted cheese, spicy mozzarella pizza, and chocolaty cheesecakes.

How delicious!

Colette knocked on the door of the first cottage. The door opened, revealing a **pleasantly plump** woman wearing an apron. Flour was sprinkled all over her clothes and face. She didn't look quite as strange or unusual as the creatures they had encountered already.

"Good afternoon, my dear," she said, smiling at Colette.

Noticing Colette's CURIOUS look, she began to brush off the flour.

"Excuse me, I'm a bit of a **mess**," she said cheerfully. "It's hard not to get dirty when you're cooking!"

"No problem," Colette said. "And I'm sorry to **DISTURB** you."

"Oh, it's no **bother**, my dear," the woman replied. Then she **LOOKED** over Colette's

Good afternoon, my dear!

shoulder. "I see that you're not alone."

"Yes, these are my **friends**," Colette said. "Pam, Nicky, Violet, Paulina, and Will. I'm Colette."

"What lovely names," she said. "I am one of the Yum Fairies."

The other fairies came out of their homes, and the friends noticed that they all had *wings*. Colette quickly counted twelve fairies. They were all plump, with different-colored hair and dresses. Each one held cooking utensils.

"Welcome!" they exclaimed together. "Now please come to the table. You're our guests!"

BON APPETIT!

Pam didn't have to be told twice. She quickly took a seat at the **TABLE**.

The other girls and Will politely thanked the **fairies** before sitting down.

"Have you had any other **guests** recently?" Colette cleverly asked.

A blonde fairy avoided Colette's eyes. "Um, yes, a lovely rodent," she said. "But she left a while ago."

Will and the Thea Sisters tried to control their **excitement**.

Did she have this?

"And did she have **THIS** with her?" Nicky asked, holding up Nina's diary.

"**Possibly**," replied a fairy, giving her a **MYSTERIOUS** smile.

"How long ago was she here?" Nicky asked.

"I'm not sure. It's difficult to keep track of time here. It comes and goes. And she came and went," said the blonde fairy, with sadness in her voice.

"Yes, alas, she didn't even stay for dinner," said another fairy, and then a **threatening** look crossed her face. "But *you* will stay."

Colette suddenly felt that the Yum Fairies might not be as nice as they looked. "Um, actually, we have to be going," she said. But when she tried to Get UP, she couldn't!

"I'm stuck!" Colette cried.

Alarmed, the others tried to stand up, too, but none of them could. It was though an INVISIBLE FORCE was keeping them glued to their seats!

"I should have known," Will said. "The fairies have caʃt a ʃpell on us!"

"It's just like what the Lake Fairies did," Nicky remarked.

"What do you want from us?" Pam asked. "Do we have to answer a **RiDDLe**?"

"It is **RUDE** to get up from a table without being served," the blonde fairy snapped. "Eat everything we have cooked for you, and you may go."

What do you want from us?

I can't get up!

Oh, no!

She waved her hand, and **HUNDREDS** of plates of food appeared, floating around them.

"We'll **never** be able to eat all this!" Paulina cried.

MYSTERIOUS MUSIC

While the Thea Sisters and Will tried to escape from the Yum Fairies, I entered the portal leading to the *Land of Erin*. I had no idea my friends were in trouble.

Agent O'Malley stayed behind to keep the fire going in the **CAVE**. I carefully descended down the stone staircase, following the sound of mysterious **music**. It seemed to be calling to me from the depths of the earth.

I walked down the *twisting* staircase for such a long time that I thought it might never end. The light from my flashlight was fading, and I began to worry.

Just in time, the space around me started to open up. The music suddenly stopped, and I glimpsed a soft GLOW in the distance.

Nina was somewhere out there. I couldn't **shake** the feeling that the agent was in some kind of **danger**.

And if that's the case, then I'll just have to find out what it is and help her, I told myself.

As I passed the final step, I saw that I was in a **CAVE**. A faint light shone from the other end, and I headed toward it.

The sparkling light grew stronger as I neared the exit, and my HEART started to beat faster. What kind of **magic** land was I about to enter? Whatever it was, I wasn't going to stop now. Closing my eyes, I stepped through the doorway into the light.

When I opened my *eyes* again, my jaw dropped. There, deep below the surface of the earth, was a marvelous forest. I could smell the sweet scents of spring in the air.

Red-and-white MUSHROOMS sprouted

from the green grass. Happy **animals** frolicked with each other, and brightly colored insects flew and hopped among the trees.

I had arrived in the Land of Erin!

A STRANGE GUIDE

I wasn't sure which way to go. Since I didn't have a map, I decided to rely on my **intuition**. I gazed around the forest, watching and listening for anything unusual.

As I concentrated, I could hear a sound in the distance: a rhythmic beat, like a **HAMMER**. Who would be using a hammer in the middle of a forest?

There was only one way to find out. I cautiously walked toward the noise, alert for any possible **DANGER**.

I could barely see the sky through the thick tree branches. But as I made my way, more **LIGHT** filtered through.

The sound of the **HAMMERING** grew louder and louder as I walked. I was brimming with curiosity. What mysterious creature

was I about to encounter?

Then I saw something very strange. The top of a giant purple **MUSHROOM** appeared ahead of me. Soon I was in a whole forest of **ENORMOUSE** mushrooms!

Among the mushrooms, a little man sat on a rock, hitting the heel of a **SHOE** with a hammer. He wore a green suit and a green top hat with a GOLD buckle.

He suddenly stopped and turned to **LOOK** at me. I guess I didn't interest him, because he turned around and continued to hammer without saying a word.

"Excuse me," I said. "My name is THEA STILTON. May I ask —"

"Good day, my fair lady!" he cried, interrupting me.

"Good day," I replied, a little startled. "May I ask who you are?"

The little man laughed. "Can't you see? I'm a LEPRECHAUN! We're SHOEMAKER PIXIES. What can I do for you?"

"I'm looking for a mouse named Nina," I said. "Maybe you've seen her?"

The leprechaun shook his head. "No, no. Definitely not. Can I do something else for you?"

"Could you show me the road toward the nearest village?" I asked.

The leprechaun grinned. "I can do better than that. I'll take you there myself!" Then he tucked the shoe and hammer in a bag and gestured for me to follow him.

Let's go!

THE GNOMES OF THE ENCHANTED FOREST

As I followed the leprechaun through the forest, a strong tremor shook the ground. "HELP! HELP! HE'S ANGRY AGAIN!" the leprechaun cried.

I turned to see who he was talking about, but I didn't see anyone — not even the leprechaun. He must have run off in **FEAR**.

Was he talking about **KING WAVESHAKER?** I wondered. There was nothing to do but continue alone. I hoped the village wasn't far, even though there was no sign of buildings on the **horizon**. So I examined the ground, looking for some tracks that might lead me there.

I quickly noticed some `tiny` footprints and thought they must be from some small forest animal. Then I looked more closely and saw that they had been made by shoes, rather than paws. Who could have such small feet? I decided to find out, and started to follow the footprints.

Now and then they would disappear, but then I would see them again, a few feet ahead. They were my best chance of finding someone who might have seen Nina.

Finally, I came to a large tree. Looking closely at the trunk, I noticed a small door carved into the base of the tree. A tiny being appeared at the door, but when it saw me it went right back inside. It seemed terrified.

Bending down, I knocked lightly at the little door. Soon, the little CREATURE reappeared.

He barely came up to my knees. He had a

gray beard, and he wore a RED CAP and POINTY little shoes. He stepped toward me cautiously, looking at me with curiosity.

"Hello," I said.

He nodded. "Hello to you, too. Tell me what you want, because I have a lot of work to do. Lots of work. We gnomes are BUSY people!"

Just then, several other gnomes came out of the trees and approached us.

"I was wondering if you could HELP me," I said as I sat on a stone to make the gnomes feel more comfortable. "I'm looking for a MOUSE."

"A fairy mouse?" the gnome asked.

I shook my head. "No, a mouse like me," I replied. "Her name is **Nina**. I haven't heard from her in a long time, and I'm worried about her."

"**Poor thing**," said the gnome. "I'm sorry, but we don't know anything about her."

"Maybe you can help me with another mystery," I said. "Do you know why King Waveshaker is so **ANGRY**?"

"I wish we knew!" the gnome replied. "The strong *WIND* he makes destroys our crops. In fact, I must get back to work right now!"

He hurried off, and a female gnome *shyly* approached me. "I seem to remember that a mouse did pass this way."

"Are you sure?" I asked, excited.

She nodded. "She had a notebook with her and . . . *this*."

She scurried away and came back holding a pen. There was an unmistakable clue on the cap: the symbol of the **Seven Roses**. This was Nina's pen!

"How long ago did you see her? And where did she go?" I asked.

"She left with the Guardians of Treasure one morning," the gnome replied. "They're **greedy** goblins who love money more than anything."

"Where can I find them?" I asked.

"They live near the **Gray Swamp**," the gnome said. "But be careful — they will surely find you first."

"And then they won't let you pass until

they've taken your GOLD," warned a bearded gnome behind her.

Before I said good-bye, I had to ask the gnome for a **favor**. "May I please have that pen?" I asked.

It was an important clue, and I thought the symbol of the Seven Roses might be helpful as I searched for Nina. I could show it to others to see if they had seen it before.

The gnome's blue eyes looked sad. "But it's mine," she said, clutching it to her chest.

I had an idea. "In exchange, I can give you this," I said, showing her the FLASHLIGHT.

The gnome didn't look impressed, so I turned the flashlight on. She smiled happily when she saw the light.

"Okay," she said, and I traded the flashlight for the pen.

The bearded **gnome** pointed past the mushroom grove. "The Gray Swamp is **THAT WAY**," he said.

I turned to **THANK** him, but he and the rest of the gnomes had all **DISAPPEARED** inside their homes. So I started walking again, wondering what I would find in the swamp.

THE GUARDIANS OF TREASURE

I quickly found the swamp — a maze of puddles of **muddy** water. The thick roots of the trees on the banks of the swamp snaked into the water, and the air smelled S A L T Y.

Which way should I go? I wondered.

I decided to stick close to the edge of the

water as I made my way around the swamp. After a few steps I heard a sound behind me — the sound of someone stepping on dry leaves and branches. Then I heard something that made me shiver: an eerie giggle!

Someone was following me, I was sure of it. My heart beat a little faster. Then I felt some drops of water on my head . . . but it wasn't raining. What was going on?

Someone is following me. . . .

I looked up and saw the tree branches rustling above me. Then I heard laughter again.

"Who's there?" I asked loudly. "Show yourself! Or are you scared?"

A group of strange creatures climbed down from the trees. They had green skin and spiky hair, and carried swords. I was a little frightened, but I didn't let them see that.

"HELLO, noble warriors," I said in my bravest voice. "What can I do for you?"

"We are the GUARDIANS OF TREASURE," one of them replied.

They had found me!

"Did you like our joke about the rain?" one of them asked.

"Forget that. Just give us your gold!" another one snapped.

"I don't have any GOLD," I replied.

The first goblin moved up close to me, eyeing me curiously.

"You remind me of someone," he said.

"Of course! She looks like the **thief**!" another goblin cried. "What was her name? It started with an **N**."

"Nina?" I guessed.

"Yes, that's it!" the goblin yelled. "She stole the GOLD that we were guarding. If we ever find her . . ."

A goblin jumped in front of him. "It's your fault that she escaped with our gold!"

It's your fault!

No, it's your fault!

"Wrong! It was your fault!" the accused goblin shot back.

More goblins joined in the argument, but I was thinking about what they said. Nina, a **thief**? That didn't make sense.

"Are you saying that Nina stole your gold?" I asked. "But that's imPOSSible!"

The Guardians of Treasure became quiet. "Of course it's possible," one spoke up. "That's why we want to find her. She's got some great skills! She stole that GOLD from right under the king's nose. We want to congratulate her."

I still couldn't believe it, but I felt like this was an important clue. "The king's gold? You mean **KING WAVESHAKER**?"

The goblins nodded. "That's why the king is so ANGRY," one replied. "He wants his gold back!"

So I had solved one part of my **myſtery**: I knew why the king was angry. But I still had to find Nina.

"Do you have any idea where I can find my friend?" I asked.

"Find the GOLD, and you'll find Nina," one of the goblins replied.

I sighed. "I got that part. But where should I look?"

"With those who are **NEVER HAPPY!**" a goblin said mysteriously.

With that, the **GUARDIANS OF TREASURE** disappeared into the swamp, and I was alone once more.

THE SAD FAIRY

I started walking again, wondering how I would get through the swampy **maze**. I couldn't stop thinking about what the Guardians of Treasure had told me, trying to make **sense** of it.

Someone had taken King Waveshaker's gold, which was why he was **unhappy**. But I knew that Nina wasn't a thief. So who really took the **GOLD**? And where was Nina? And who were "those who are never happy"?

Something told me that once I solved the mystery of the **STOLEN** treasure, I would find Nina.

Then a distant **SOUND** interrupted my thoughts. I stopped, listening. It sounded like someone **crying**.

Could this have something to do with

Nina? I hurried in the direction of the cries. I soon reached the entrance to a wide cave covered in creeping plants. The crying was definitely coming from inside.

I hesitated. The air coming from the cave was cold and damp. It was **dark** in there, and I didn't have my flashlight. But I knew I had to investigate.

My eyes adjusted to the darkness as I

A cave!

made my way through the cave. I could make out a shape in the distance.

"**Nina?**" I called out.

But whoever it was just kept crying.

"**Nina?**" I repeated.

I moved closer, and a crack in the ceiling of the cave let in a sliver of **LIGHT** so I could see the crying figure better. It wasn't Nina — it was a fairy with BLUE hair, a dress made of plants, and pale pink **wings**.

I stared, enchanted. Before I came to the Land of Erin, I had only read about fairy creatures in stories. Now I was seeing them up close, and each was more incredible than the last.

The fairy was still sobbing.

"Can I help you?" I asked.

The fairy didn't respond, but I kept trying. "Excuse me," I said, "I don't mean to disturb

you, but I heard you **CRYING**, and I thought I'd come closer."

The fairy just cried even **LOUDER**. I took a few steps closer, and she drew back from me.

"What do you want?" she asked.

"I just want to **help** you," I said. "Why are you crying?"

She stared at me with eyes that shone like jewels. But she looked **SAD**, and I intended to find out why.

"You aren't from here, and you don't know who I am," she replied. Her voice was musical and cracked with emotion when she spoke.

"That's true," I admitted. "I come from very far away. And I don't know who you are."

"I am a **banshee**, a fairy of the hills,"

she explained.

"Why are you here, all alone in a cave?" I asked.

"It is my *destiny* to be sad," she said, and then burst into tears once more.

"That's terrible!" I cried. "No one should be destined for sadness."

"We banshees are," she explained. "But I don't like crying in front of everyone, so I hide myself in this cave."

I felt bad for the fairy, but I had an IDEA that might cheer her up: I would tell her a joke! If she had spent her whole life in this cave, she might never have heard one before. But what kind of joke would a fairy like? I thought for a moment . . .

and then the inspiration came to me.

"Would you like to hear a $funny$ story?" I asked.

The fairy's long, pointy ears perked up, and she nodded, still sobbing.

"Two pixies were talking," I began. "One **PIXIE** said to the other, 'What kind of **ROOM** does a fairy like best?' The other pixie thought, but was stumped. The first pixie said, 'A **MUSHROOM**!'"

Ha, ha, ha!

At first, the banshee gave me a blank look, but a few seconds later, a $smile$ formed on her lips. Then she laughed, softly at first, but then really hard, as if she had been waiting her whole life to **LaUGH**.

Her laugh sounded light and beautiful, like lovely music. I laughed with her.

"Thank you," she said once she had recovered. "I haven't had a reason to laugh before now. You've filled my heart with **JOY**!"

"There's a first time for everything, even new FEELINGS," I replied.

The fairy smiled. "That's true. I thought my destiny didn't include joy, until now."

Then she took the necklace of flowers off her neck and handed it to me. "This is for you."

"Thank you," I said. "It's beautiful."

"It's not just a simple **NECKLACE**," the fairy added. "If you close your eyes, ask a question, and then BREATHE in the flowers' fragrance, the answer will come to you. You must be careful, though: Every time you ask a question, the flowers will 𝓌𝒾𝓁𝓉 and will eventually die."

"I don't know how to thank you," I said. I was truly moved. "But now I must be on my way."

She smiled at me, and I found myself 𝓈𝓂𝒾𝓁𝒾𝓃𝓰 as I got back on the path.

THAT SMiLE WAS THE BEST GiFT SHE COULD HAVE GiVEN ME!

A STRANGE TABLE

When I left the cave, I touched the flower **PETALS** on the necklace. As the fairy instructed, I closed my eyes and asked, "Nina, where are you?"

As I breathed in the delicate scent of the flowers, a **CRYSTAL CLEAR** image appeared in my mind. I saw Nina, trapped in a cage of thorny branches!

"Nina!" I cried. "You're being held **prisoner**!" But **WHO** had captured her? And where could she be?

Although I was tempted to ask the **necklace** these questions, I decided

to wait. A few flowers had already wilted, and I wanted to save the powers of the necklace in case of an **EMERGENCY**.

So I walked into the forest, and soon I smelled BURNING wood in the air. I looked over the treetops and saw smoke in the distance. Maybe it was a village!

I walked faster and quickly reached a **GROUP** of small creatures with green skin. Each one had a **bell** around his neck, and I guessed that they were probably pixies. They seemed to be arguing.

"It's all his fault that we're **lost** again," said one, pointing to the pixie next to him. "Now we're hungrier than ever!"

"I was just following the SMOKE," the accused pixie protested.

Another pixie groaned. "We need to find some food, fast!"

One of the pixies noticed me. He smacked his friends, and they all turned and **ſtared** at me.

"Did you lose your **GROUP**, too?" one of them asked.

I didn't understand. "What group?"

"A group of strange, **furry** creatures like you," he replied.

"Are you saying that you've seen others who look like me?" I asked.

What group?

They all nodded. **"EXACTLY!"**

One of the pixies got a dreamy look in his eyes. "The **blonde** one was so cute."

"And the red-haired one was funny," said another. "Oh, and don't forget the one with the long black hair. She was pretty serious."

"And there was a dark-haired one who was very **NICE**," another pixie added. "And one with **curly** brown hair. She was funny, too."

The **pixies** laughed, remembering. I couldn't believe what they had just told me. It sounded like they were describing the **THEA SISTERS!**

"So there were **FIVE** in the group?" I asked.

"Oh, I don't remember," one of the pixies said. "I'm too hungry to think!"

"There was a **BRAVE** young rodent

with them," one of the pixies remembered. "He wore a **red** jacket."

They had to be talking about my five friends. But who was the rodent with them? Then it hit me — they must have decided to **follow** me once their exams were done. They probably contacted the **I.I.S.**, which meant that Will Mystery was with them!

I **ABSOLUTELY** had to find them.

"Do you know where they are now?" I asked.

"We were all heading that way, toward the SMOKE, but then we got lost," one of the pixies said.

"Can you please show me the way?" I asked.

"Of course! We love to GUIDE visitors through the forest!" the pixie said.

And they headed off down the path, their

bells **JINGLING**.

Now, I didn't know that the pixies had a knack for getting lost. But I got **lucky**, because they took me right to the source of the smoke. When we emerged from the trees, I was speechless.

There, sitting around a dining table filled with food, were the **THEA SISTERS** and **WILL MYSTERY**!

I ran to the table, my heart beating with **JOY**.

"Thea!" Violet exclaimed.

"Don't sit down!" Will Mystery warned me. "We're **prisoners** at this table. The Yum Fairies trapped us here with a spell. We can't leave unless we finish *eating* all the food they've made."

"And there's so much food even *I* can't eat it," Pam moaned.

"That's terrible!" I exclaimed. "Where are these Yum Fairies?"

Then I heard a voice behind me.

"Hello, my good lady!"

I turned and saw a plump gray-haired fairy wearing an apron over her blue dress. Lacy pink **WiNGS** fluttered on her back.

"Are you a friend of these dear rodents?" she asked. "We've made a delicious **lunch** for them. Would you care to sit down?"

More Yum Fairies had appeared and were PILING food on the plates of their reluctant guests. I felt so bad for all of them. *What a strange situation!*

A CLEVER SOLUTION

I didn't know how to refuse the fairy's **INVITATION**, so I responded as politely as I could. "Thank you, *kind fairy*, but I've already had lunch."

"Oh, no, dear. You must sit down!" the fairy insisted.

Then **Colette** asked for more food, distracting her. Paulina opened up a **notebook** and motioned for me to read:

Yum Fairies **NEVER** sit down at their table. Their guests are kept as prisoners until all of the food is gone. However, one guest can take the place of another.

So the only way out of this **MESS** was to find six other guests who could take the place of my friends.

Then it hit me. "I have an IDEA," I whispered to Paulina. "I met some very hungry pixies in the forest."

"You mean the GREEN PIXIES?" Paulina whispered back. "We thought they were lost."

I looked behind me, but I didn't see them. WHERE had they gone?

One of the Yum Fairies flew right up to me. "You really must sit down, my dear," she said sternly, waving her ROLLING PIN.

I pushed past her, but the other fairies flew in front of me, trying to block my way. I quickly DODGED them and raced into the forest.

"I'll be right back!" I called out.

Some of them flew after me anyway.

"*STOP!*" they yelled.

Luckily, I quickly found the Green Pixies playing in the trees.

"There you are!" I exclaimed.

They stared at me in SURPRISE.

"And here *you* are," one of them said. "We thought you were over tHeRe." He pointed in the opposite direction from where I had come.

Here you are!

"Well, I'm here now," I said. "Are you pixies still hungry?"

"Yes, very!"

"Then come with me," I said.

The Yum Fairies followed us, suspicious. But when we got back to the dining table, the Green Pixies RUSHED toward the food. They began to talk at once.

"It smells so **delicious**!"

"Can we eat?"

"Can we sit down?"

The Yum Fairies were delighted. "Of course! Please have a seat."

"They can take our PLACES," Colette said quickly.

The gray-haired fairy frowned. "But you can't leave so soon."

"We know the rules," Paulina said firmly. "These Green Pixies can substitute for us."

"**YES! YES!**" agreed the hungry pixies. The Yum Fairies couldn't object.

"Very well," said the gray-haired fairy.

Will and the Thea Sisters tried to stand — and this time, it worked.

"**HOORAY! HOORAY!**" they cheered.

The Yum Fairies looked sad. Even though the Thea Sisters had been tricked, they felt **bad** for the fairy cooks.

"We're very sorry that we can't stay," Violet said. "The food was quite delicious."

"You are always **WELCOME** at our table," the gray-haired fairy said.

Then we all quickly left the grove of the Yum Fairies. Behind us, we could hear the Green Pixies digging into the feast.

"**Yum! Yum! Yum!**"

TOGETHER AGAIN!

I was so **HaPPY** that I had found the Thea Sisters and Will, I almost thought I was dreaming. Now we could look for Nina, and figure out who stole Waveshaker's gold!

We walked through the forest, **CHATTING.** We had plenty of things to tell each other!

"We **contacted** the I.I.S. because we thought you might need our **help**," Nicky admitted.

"I'm glad you did," I said. "Traveling in this **enCHanteD** world on my own hasn't been easy. But how did you get here?"

"There are many projects in the Seven Roses Unit that you don't know about yet," Will replied. "Like the **secret portal**."

"Portal? Is that how you got here?" I asked.

Will nodded. "Through the portal, we can travel to other dimensions in **SPACE AND TIME**, including all of the fantasy worlds."

"**Incredible!**" I exclaimed. "I never imagined that your research would have taken you so far."

"And I can guess how you got here," Will said. "Through the secret passage in the **ruins** of the castle, right?"

Look, Thea!

"How did you know?" I asked. Paulina answered for him. "After we arrived in Erin, we **FOUND** this," she explained, passing me the **DIARY** she had shown me before. "It's Nina's. She took notes while she was exploring, and it contains a lot of useful **information**!"

I nodded. Everything was much clearer.

"I've been on Nina's trail," I said. "She met all kinds of amazing creatures. Then I learned something that's got me *worried*."

"What happened to her?" Violet asked anxiously.

I told them about the *flower* necklace that the banshee had given me, and the vision it had showed me.

"Nina has been **CAPTURED**, but I don't know by whom," I said.

The mouselets gasped.

"I also discovered why King Waveshaker is angry," I reported. "Someone **stole** his GOLD, and Nina has been accused of the theft."

Will nodded. "That makes sense," he said. "Thea, you should know that the king's ANGER is putting this world in grave danger. There is a **crack** on the map in the Hall of the Seven Roses."

"I haven't been to the hall yet," I reminded him. "What kind of **map** is this?"

"The hall contains maps of each fantasy world," Will **explained**. "Each one is connected to the MAGNETIC WAVES of the **land** it represents. If something happens to the map, we know there's trouble."

I listened, spellbound.

"A **crack** appeared in the map right after

the Thea Sisters arrived at the I.I.S.," Will said. "We knew we had to act fast, before it got worse."

"Then Will asked us to come with him, and of course we said yes," Paulina reported.

I was proud of my brave students. They never backed down from a challenge!

"Let me tell you about the Guardians of Treasure," I said, and I told them what they had said about Nina. "They told me to search for 'those who are NEVER HAPPY' if I wanted to find her."

Violet looked startled. "The Lake Fairies told us something similar. They said to look out for 'the depths of an unhappy heart.'"

"There might be a CLUE in the diary," Paulina suggested. "But some of the pages are torn and stained."

We studied the pages, and then we saw an

underlined note: *Court . . . the . . . Disc . . ented . . . Valley of Wi . . . es.*

"Maybe it's 'Court of the Discontented,'" I guessed. "*Discontented* means 'unhappy.'"

"And I bet it's in the **Valley of Wishes**," Paulina said, pointing to the line.

Will opened the map. "You're right! There is a Valley of Wishes on the map. **Well done!** But it looks rather far away."

It was time to use the **necklace** again. I closed my eyes and asked for the quickest way to the valley, and I saw a clear picture of the route in my mind.

When I opened my eyes, the Thea Sisters were in a **panic**.

"Pam has disappeared!" Colette cried.

"How did that happen?" I asked.

"Pam! Pam!" Nicky yelled. But she didn't reply. Pam seemed to have VANISHED into thin air.

"Where did she go?" Colette asked anxiously.

"We'll find her," I said confidently. "There's got to be an explanation."

I looked at my necklace and closed my eyes.

"Where is Pam?" I asked.

But this time I didn't get a vision. The flowers were all WILTED, and I realized that I might have used up their magic.

Discouraged, I looked at Will.

"We'll split up," he suggested. "You take the rest of the Thea Sisters to the Valley of Wishes, and I'll look for Pam. We'll catch up to you, *I promise!*"

WAVESHAKER RUMBLES

Colette, Nicky, Paulina, Violet, and I headed toward the **valley of Wishes**. As we walked, the earth started to **shake** beneath our feet.

"We need to find our way out of this forest!" I shouted. "The **tRees** could fall at any moment!"

At that moment, a **herd** of small woodland animals ran past us.

"Let's follow them!" Nicky suggested. "They must know a way out."

We ran after them as fast as we could as tree branches **crashed** down all around us.

Hearts pounding, we reached the edge of the forest just as the **shaking** stopped.

"**WE'RE SAFE!**" Paulina said. "I just hope that Will and Pam are okay."

We surveyed the scene. The trees opened up onto a beautiful **lake** bordered by a valley. Purple mountain peaks rose on the far shore.

I recognized the place immediately from the vision the necklace had showed me. It was the **Valley of Wishes**!

"We can walk around the **lake**," I said.

The mouselets smiled at me **confidently**, and we set off for the mountains.

TED'S DILEMMA

While I made my way to the Valley of Wishes, Agent Ted O'Malley remained in the cave back in Ireland. He had an important job to do. If the FIRE burning in the cave went out, the door to the Land of Erin would close — and I would be **TRAPPED** there.

Tending the fire was no easy task. Ted waited for me for **hours and hours**, and soon he began to grow tired. **ZZZZZZZZZ**. Ted dozed off, snoring quietly. But a few minutes later, a horrible loud noise woke him up.

The sound seemed to come from the depths of the earth,

and the walls of the cave **shook**. A cold wind *whipped* through the cave. Since he was a seasoned agent, Ted remained **calm**. He threw a few more branches on the fire so it wouldn't go out.

Then the trembling stopped, and the wind died down. Ted smiled. The **WORST** was over!

Relieved, Ted got up and walked to the mouth of the cave. What he saw wiped the smile off his face. High waves crashed against the cliffs, and dark, heavy clouds filled the sky.

"Hmm . . . I don't like this sudden calm," he mused.

He walked back to the fire just as another violent *GUST OF WIND* blew through the cave. He watched, horrified, as the flames went out! He looked down and saw that the portal to the Land of Erin had slid shut.

"Oh, no! This can't be!" he wailed.

Frantically, he tried to relight the fire, but the winds were too strong. *Thea is TRAPPED!* he thought.

The storm was raging now. The **CRASHING** waves pushed water inside the cave. Soon, Ted knew, the cave would be **flooded**.

It's useless to try to keep lighting the fire,

he realized. *If I don't leave now, it may be* **TOO LATE**. *I need to inform the I.I.S. of this new development!*

Ted looked down at the floor of the cave one last time, and his heart felt **HEAVY**. He hated to leave me behind.

It's the only way, Ted told himself. *If I can get out of here safely, I can let the I.I.S. know what has happened to Thea Stilton. They*

Oh, no! It can't be!

might know some other way to save her.

His mind made up, Ted walked through the cave and back into the **ruins** of the castle, and then found the small boat that we had used to reach the island. The sea was rough, but he was a seasoned sailor. He pushed offshore and into the **stormy** waters.

A BAD OMEN

It was already getting **dark** when the mouselets and I reached the Valley of Wishes. We started to climb up the mountainside, and soon we spotted a small VILLAGE in the distance.

"Do you think that could be the Court of the Discontented?" Colette asked.

Paulina flipped through Nina's diary. "Nina describes it as a group of ROCKY huts, located near the start of the valley, along the banks of a river. I think the description matches. Then the DIARY ends. So this could be the last place Nina visited before she LOST her diary," she reasoned.

"Maybe the members of the court are the ones who stole Waveshaker's GOLD," Violet suggested.

"It's possible, but it's also possible that Nina ran into some other fairies, who stole the gold," I said. "We need to find more clues."

"So let's go!" Nicky said eagerly.

"We need to be careful," I reminded them. "We don't know what we'll find out there. If the Discontented did **steal** the gold, they'll fight for it, and probably won't be very friendly."

The Thea Sisters nodded, and we moved forward, but it was getting harder to see in the **dark**. Nicky had the idea to make TORCHES from tree branches, and she gave one to each of us.

"**FANTASTIC!**" we cried at once.

We had finally reached the outskirts of the village when I heard footsteps nearby.

I stopped. Had we walked right into a **tRaP**? But it was too late.

A group of strange creatures carrying **axes** quickly surrounded us. They were large and smelled of dirt. Each one wore a red cap on top of his **shaggy** hair.

Who are you?

The Thea Sisters looked terrified, and I realized that I needed to keep everyone calm.

"May I ask who you are?" I said without any **FEAR** in my voice.

One of them stepped up to me, staring at me with fierce black eyes.

"We are the **Red Caps**," he said, "from the Court of the Discontented."

Another one approached me. "**FOLLOW US!**" he barked in an **EVIL** voice. "And don't even bother to resist!"

We silently obeyed as the creatures pushed us forward.

THE COURT OF THE DISCONTENTED

The Red Caps **marched** us through the valley, toward the river. I could see the Thea Sisters casting nervous glances at each other. What was going to happen to us?

When we reached the **river**, the leader of the group took us across a narrow **BRIDGE** that crossed the rough water. As soon as we reached the other shore, we heard a strange crying sound coming from the river.

What, or who, could that be?

I tried to see where the Red Caps had taken us. We seemed to be outside a circle of ramshackle huts illuminated by a BONFIRE in the center. Past the huts, I could make out the shape of a large, **DARK** building.

"It looks like a castle!" Nicky cried.

The castle looked **terrifying**, with tall towers and a forbidding front gate. And the Red Caps were leading us right toward it!

A **sad cry** rose up from the river once again.

"What is that noise?" I bravely asked.

The leader of the Red Caps answered me. "It's the voice of the **Sad Washerwoman**."

"Who is that?" I asked, curious.

"Her spirit is held **prisoner** in the

Woe is me....

water," the leader explained. "She must spend her days washing clothes and crying over her fate."

"There aren't any happy people in this land," Colette observed, looking around.

"Of course not!" snapped one of the Red Caps. "We're in the Court of the Discontented, after all!"

They continued to lead us to the castle, and all of the creatures we passed looked SAD and **AFRAID**, too.

"Let's go! That's enough talking!" one of the Red Caps barked.

I gave my friends a comforting smile as

We're here!

our captors led us through the menacing castle **gate**.

The gate led into a long, **DARK** hallway. We walked along, prodded by the Red Caps, until the hall opened up into a **LARGE ROOM**.

Someone was waiting for us there. . . .

JUST ONE MORE . . .

When the Thea Sisters and I headed off to find the Court of the Discontented, Will headed into the *forest* to find Pam.

When it got dark, he lit a *TORCH*, and Pam spotted it.

"Will!" she cried out.

He turned and saw Pam in the *shadows*. She looked lost and afraid.

Will ran up to her. "What happened to you? We were worried."

"I'm sorry," Pam replied, embarrassed. "A delicious **SMELL**

Pam!

hit my nose, and for some reason I couldn't **STOP** myself from following it. I went off to find it without letting anyone know."

"We called out for you. Didn't you hear us?" Will asked.

"All I could think about was the sweet-smelling fruit," Pam said. "It's like I became some kind of zombie. I found it and quickly ate some, and then I couldn't remember who I was, or where I was."

Will frowned. "Which FRUIT?"

"Follow me," Pam said.

She led Will to a tree with a thick trunk and gnarled **branches** that reached down like snakes.

Will stepped closer. Each branch dripped with **plump**, red fruit.

Pam reached out to take a piece, but Will quickly stopped her.

"Wait! I've read about this fruit!" he cried. "They're the **FRUIT OF FORGETFULNESS**, and they're very dangerous. If you eat them, they make you lose your memory. Luckily, it's only temporary."

But Pam was still under their **spell**. She reached out again.

"Just one more," she pleaded.

"**No, you mustn't!**" Will yelled, grabbing her arm.

Pam gave the tree a longing look. Then she turned to Will.

"You're right," she said. "I can **RESIST** them, I promise."

Will let go, and Pam gave the berries one last look, but she didn't give in.

"**Whew!**" she exclaimed in relief. "I

think the spell is broken. Thank you."

"No problem," Will replied. "It's a good thing I recognized the fruit, or I might have been caught in the **SPELL**, too."

Pam smiled at Will gratefully. "How are my friends? And Thea?"

"Fine, as far as I know," Will replied. "We split up so I could look for you. We'd better get moving so we can **join** them."

"Where did they go?" Pam asked.

"To the Valley of Wishes, to find the Court of the Discontented," Will **explained**. "Following a **clue** from Nina's diary."

Pam looked up at the **NIGHT** sky, alarmed.

"Don't worry, we'll find the way," Will assured her. "I have a great sense of direction, even in the dark."

Pam **sighed** with relief. "Thanks for coming

to find me. I'd still be lost." She shivered.

"Let's go!" Will said, smiling.

Darkness covered the forest like a GHOSTLY cloak, but Will's **torch** lit the way. The pair made their way through the FOREST, eager to find their friends.

They got **LOST** several times, but **HOURS** later, they finally reached the VALLEY OF WISHES.

"I see LIGHTS!"

I see lights!

Pam cried, pointing into the valley.

"They must be coming from the **Court of the Discontented**," Will guessed. "The map doesn't show any other villages around here."

"We should **HURRY** and try to find everyone," Pam said.

"First, let's come up with a **PLAN**," Will suggested.

"Why do we need a plan?" Pam asked.

"This place is called the Court of the Discontented, after all," Will pointed out. "So I'm guessing that they're **not very friendly**. And we have no idea how they've greeted Thea and the others. They might be in some kind of **trouble**. I don't like the looks of this place."

Pam nodded. "You're right. So what should we do?"

Will thought for a moment. "We can put out this TORCH, to start. Then we can try to sneak in without being seen."

Pam nodded. "This way, if the others are in trouble, we can help them."

"Exactly," Will said. "We must be ready for any POSSIBILITY."

He put out the torch. "Stay close so we don't lose each other."

She didn't respond, but Will heard her move forward in the DARKNESS behind him.

THE GREAT DISCONTENTED ONE

Meanwhile, the mouselets and I entered the dark room in the forbidding castle.

"**Come forward!**" a deep voice demanded, and we saw a large, shadowy figure seated on a throne.

Since none of us moved right away, one of the Red Caps **PRODDED** me with his spear. I took his hint and stepped toward the throne.

"Who are you?" the huge creature **bellowed**.

Before I could answer, he rose to his feet. He was **ENORMOUSE**! His face looked as if it had been carved from a mountain, and it was covered by a dark, **shaggy** beard.

His dark eyes were **cold** and **ruthless**,

and I knew that we must have found the leader of the Discontented Ones.

"Your Majesty, what do you want from us?" I asked politely but calmly.

"I will be the one to ask QUESTIONS," he replied menacingly.

"As you wish," I replied evenly. He was trying to intimidate me, but I wasn't going to let him.

"I am the **Great Discontented One**, the ruler of this court," he announced. "Nobody pokes their noses into my realm without permission!"

"We weren't **POKING** our noses into anything!" Nicky protested.

"And we weren't in your **realm**," Paulina added.

"**OH, REALLY?**" he bellowed, turning to his guards.

They took a step backward. "Well, they were on the b-b-border," one of them stammered.

"Humph!" said their leader. "In any case, you are **STRANGERS**, and you're not even from this world!"

I interrupted him. "We are looking for a **mouse**, and we won't

I don't want strangers here!

leave until we find her," I said firmly.

"And what makes you think she might be here, this . . . **MOUSE**?" the leader asked.

"So she's not here?" I asked.

"Do not respond to my **question** with another **QUESTION**!" he fumed.

"Well, we think that she is here," I insisted.

"So you are here to find a mouse," the leader said, rubbing his beard. "All right, I will allow it, since I'm in a good mood today. Isn't that right, my faithful ones?"

We're looking for a mouse!

"YES!" the Red Caps all exclaimed.

Their leader sighed with satisfaction. But I didn't trust this Great Discontented One. Convincing him to take us to our friend had been too easy.

Still, we had no choice but to follow the Red Caps and the Great Discontented One. I was feeling pretty sure that they had Nina, and this might be our only chance to **RESCUE** her.

They led us into the castle courtyard, where a fire was burning. The flames illuminated a mouse . . . a mouse held prisoner in **A CAGE MADE OF BRAMBLES**!

NOW WHAT?

"**Nina!**" I exclaimed.

The young rodent looked in my direction, and her eyes lit up.

"You know me?" she asked, surprised.

I drew as close as I could, then leaned forward and whispered to her.

"My name is Thea Stilton, and these are the Thea Sisters. We've been **working** with the **SEVEN ROSES UNIT**," I explained, showing her my rose-shaped crystal pendant. "Will Mystery was **worried** about you, and we came to look for you."

Then I **TURNED** to their leader. "Your Majesty, why have you imprisoned her? That's not a very nice thing to do."

"I don't do very **NICE** things!" he **THUNDERED** in reply.

He stomped toward me. "I am the Great Discontented One, and I rule with **sadness** and **FRUSTRATION!**"

"Relcase this mouse immediately!" Colette demanded angrily.

"I will do better than that, my dear," the ruler replied. "Since you are so close with her, I will let you **rot** in prison right along with her!"

"**WHAT?**" I exclaimed.

"You heard me," he said cruelly. Then he barked to his guards. "Hurry up! Build another **CAGE!**"

Some of the Red Caps **SURROUNDED** us while the others worked to build the

Grunt!

cage. It was a **ridiculous situation**: We had finally found Nina, but now we couldn't leave!

There was nothing we could do. They quickly stuck us inside the **BRAMBLES**.

"You can't **escape**!" the leader bragged. "There is no way to unravel the tangled branches from the inside."

Ha, ha, ha!

Then he burst into **WICKED** laughter.
"You are my prisoners . . . forever!" he cried,
and then he stomped away.

! WE WERE TRAPPED! !

Our only hope was Will Mystery and Pam.
If they had followed our **tracks**,
they might be able to help us.

"I'm so sorry," Nina said
with a sigh.

"Don't **APOLOGIZE**," I
said. "It's not your fault."

"But if you hadn't come to
look for me, you wouldn't be in this
mess right now!" she pointed out.

"We're glad that we found you," I said.
"And now that we're together, I'm sure we'll
find a way out of this . . . **THORNY**
situation."

Nina smiled at the joke.

"How did you find out where I was?" she asked.

Paulina held up the **DIARY**. "We found this."

"It's a little **damaged**, but it led us right to you," Violet told her.

"But why did you come here, to the Court of the Discontented?" Colette asked. "It seems like a ***dangerous*** place to come to all by yourself."

Nina shot a look at the Red Caps who were guarding us. They had fallen asleep and were *snoring* loudly.

"I'll tell you everything," she said.

PRECIOUS HELP

As we got ready to hear Nina's story, Will and Pam reached the RIVER in the Valley of Wishes.

They both felt relieved. They had become lost so often in the dark, but now it looked like they were finally close.

"This river should take us to the **Court of the Diſcontented**," Will said.

"If only we knew exactly where Thea and the others were," Pam remarked.

Listen!

"**Liſten!**" Will said. "I hear something."

Pam didn't hear anything, and she watched, curious, as Will went to the river and began to sing a **STRANGE MELODY**. Then she heard a sound like a woman wailing.

The surface of the river rippled and a woman's face **blossomed** on the surface. She seemed to be made of **water**, and she spoke to Will in a language Pam had never heard before. To Pam's amazement, Will answered her in the same language.

"Will, what's happening?" Pam asked.

"She is the **Sad Washerwoman**, a spirit of the water," he explained. "She asked me what we're doing here. I told her, and she wants to help us."

"But how can you **UNDERSTAND** her?" Pam asked.

"In the Seven Roses Unit, we study the **LANGUAGES** spoken in the fantasy worlds," he informed her.

Pam nodded. "Can you ask her if she knows where **THEA** and the others are?"

Will sang again, and the spirit sang back to him.

"She said that the **Red Caps**, who are known to be bullies, passed here with a group of creatures who looked like us," he reported.

"And where did they take them?" Pam asked.

"To the **castle** past the village," Will replied. "Home of the Court of the Discontented."

"Then Thea and the others might be prisoners!" Pam cried in alarm.

Will nodded. "I'm afraid so. The **SPIRIT** says we should follow the river so we won't be captured, too."

"She is very **kind**," Pam remarked.

Then Will sang again, and the spirit disappeared into the WATER.

"I thanked the **Sad Washerwoman** for helping us," Will told Pam, "and now we must **get going**."

Pam followed him, impressed. They **quietly** walked along the banks of the river until they reached the village. All was still, and it was likely that everyone was asleep.

"Do you think the castle is watched by GUARDS?" Pam asked.

"Most likely," Will guessed. "We must try to get in without them spotting us."

They moved **CAUTIOUSLY** along the village walls, dodging the torchlight, until they reached the castle.

The sound of someone **snoring** could be heard from the courtyard.

"Cheese and crackers!" Pam exclaimed. "Maybe the guard over there has fallen asleep!"

They headed toward the courtyard, where they could see a **fire** burning. As they got closer, they saw two large **BRAMBLE CAGES** . . . the cages holding us prisoner!

I see two cages!

NINA'S STORY

In the meantime, before Will and Pam arrived, Nina told us her story.

"My assignment at the I.I.S. was to research the **𝓛and of 𝓔rin** so we could add more details to the **map** in the Hall of the Seven Roses," she began. "I immediately began to study every **document** we had in the department's library. In one very old book, I discovered that there was a **LINK** to Erin in Ireland. This was very **EXCITING**! Until then, we were convinced that the **SECRET PORTAL** in the I.I.S. was the only link to these fantasy worlds. So of course I had to travel to Ireland myself, to see if it was true."

"How did you discover the exact location of the **passageway**?" Paulina asked, curious.

"I began by **INTERVIEWING** the sailors and the oldest inhabitants along the coast, collecting their stories," she explained. "In Dunmore East, they told me an interesting legend about a ruined castle that contained a **mysterious stairway**. I had a feeling that the stairway might be the passage I had read about."

I nodded. "I used that same stairway to enter the *Land of Erin*."

"Great work finding it," Nina complimented me.

"Thanks," I said. "Agent O'Malley helped me find it. He knew where you were headed, and after you went **MISSING**, he regretted not going with you."

"I was too **excited** to wait for backup," Nina admitted. "And as you can see, it got me into some trouble."

"How did you end up in the Court of the Discontented?" Nicky asked.

Nina sighed. "I came to Erin knowing many **secrets**, and the more I explored, the more I learned," she explained. "Word spread quickly about a **STRANGE** furry creature who knew secrets, and the **Great Discontented One** sent his Red Caps after me."

"They wanted information?" I asked.

Nina nodded. "They **CAPTURED** me and demanded I reveal everything I knew about Erin. I did, hoping that they would let me go. They were very interested in my stories about **KING WAVESHAKER** and his wealth. They decided to steal the king's treasure, and they succeeded."

"I don't understand," Colette said. "They learned your secrets, and they got the

TREASURE they wanted. So why haven't they let you go?"

A cloud came over Nina's face. "That's the really **SCARY** part. They want me to help them **LEAVE** the Land of Erin."

"Why would they want to do that?" I asked.

"They're afraid that King Waveshaker will send his guards to get the treasure back, once he finds out they **stole** it," Nina explained. "They think they will be safe in our world."

"**That's terrible!**" Nicky exclaimed. "Can you imagine what those Red Caps would do in our world?"

"And what those in our world would do if they found out about the *Land of Erin*?" Paulina asked.

I nodded. "These Discontented Ones are putting both of our worlds in **DANGER**.

And besides that, they have made King Waveshaker very **angry**."

Nina nodded. "Yes, I've felt the earth **tremble** here."

"His anger has caused a **crack** in the map in the Hall of the Seven Roses," I informed her, and then I told her how the Thea Sisters had arrived in Erin, leading up to Pam's disappearance. "The good thing, though, is that Will and Pam are out there somewhere. I'm sure they'll arrive soon to **HELP** us."

At that moment, we heard a sound coming from outside the courtyard.

FOOTSTEPS!

GOOD MORNING!

The sound of **footsteps** came closer, but we still couldn't see anyone. We held our breath, waiting, until we heard a voice whisper.

"Thea?" It was Pam. She and Will had arrived to free us!

When Will saw Nina, his face lit up with happiness. "**Nina!** We've finally found you. Are you okay?"

"I'm fine, Will," Nina whispered through the branches. "I'm glad you're here, but the Red Caps will be awake any minute. They gather at **DAWN** every morning to go hunting. Before leaving, they make their rounds through the village and leave a few behind to stand guard. So you must hide!"

"When the coast is clear, we'll find a way

to escape," I added.

Pam and Will disappeared into the SHADOWS just in time! The Red Cap who was **guarding** us was just opening his eyes.

Just in time!

"Good morning! Sleep well?" Nicky asked, trying to sound cheerful.

He turned a sleepy eye toward her and yawned. "I **SLEPT HORRIBLY**, as usual," he muttered unhappily.

"Can we please have some **water**?" Nicky asked.

Laughing, the guard took a small horn out of his pocket and blew into it. A few seconds later, a second LAZY Red Cap appeared.

"**THEY WANT A DRINK**," the first guard said. The other one left and returned a

minute later with a jug
of water. I took a sip
but had to spit it out. It had
an **awful taste**!

"Yep! Everything is **BAD** here,
even the taste of the water," the
second Red Cap said gloomily.

Anything else?

"Hey, send someone to take my place," **GRUMBLED** the one guarding us. "I'm tired of staying here."

Just then, a third guard showed up. He was **grumbling**, too. "I don't understand why it's my turn again. I stood guard yesterday.

IT'S NOT FAIR! I'M NOT HAPPY! NOT HAPPY AT ALL!"

I understood why they called these creatures the Discontented Ones. They spent all their time **complaining**, without being able to see the good in the world.

The guards switched places, and we saw a group of Red Caps leaving the castle to go hunting, just as Nina had told us. Soon, the court would be mostly empty, giving us our only chance to escape!

HELP . . .
FROM THE SKY!

Will and Pam didn't wait to make their move. They **BOLDLY** marched up to the lone Red Cap left to guard us.

"Stop right there!" he barked, pointing his **spear** at them. "Who are you? What do you want?"

"You will free our friends right now!" Will ordered him.

I wondered what Will was up to. Did he really expect the guard to give in?

The Red Cap chuckled. "Sorry, I can't do that. In fact, you'll be joining them inside their cages." Then he charged right at them!

At that moment, Will **sang** out a strange cry — first very high-pitched, then very low. Suddenly, hundreds of birds appeared in the sky, **CIRCLING** right over us. There were so many that they completely blocked out the **SUNLIGHT**.

Terrified, the Red Cap turned as **pale** as mozzarella and ran off.

Then the **birds** swooped down and began to pull at the tangled branches with their **BEAKS**. They swiftly **unknotted** the cages. We were free!

I had never seen anything so surprising.

"How . . . how did you do that?" Paulina asked, clearly **STUNNED**.

"I asked these birds to

HELP us, and they were happy to do it," Will explained. But the Thea Sisters still looked shocked. "As I've already told Pam, in the Seven Roses Unit we study the LANGUAGES of all of the creatures in these fantasy worlds. I'm just lucky that I'm fluent in the language of fairy birds."

Paulina **shook** her head. "You are **AMAZING**!"

"I didn't do anything — it was all them," Will said, looking up at the sky. **"THANK YOU, MY FRIENDS!"**

The incredible birds seemed to understand Will, and they flew back up into the sky, blanketing it with their **RAINBOW** colors. It was a spectacular sight!

I hated to disrupt the magic of the moment, but even though we had found Nina, our work wasn't done. Until we **found**

Waveshaker's **treasure** and returned it to him, the Land of Erin was in **danger**.

"Sorry, everyone, but we've got to get moving," I said. *"First, we'll find the treasure, and then we can stop Waveshaker!"*

"I know where the Great Discontented One has **HIDDEN** it," Nina said quickly. "Let's not waste time. The Red Caps will

return in an hour or two, and once we have the **TREASURE** we'll need to get as far away as possible. Quick, come with me!"

So we all followed her inside the dark, crumbling CASTLE. . . .

WAVESHAKER'S TREASURE!

Nina guided us through the **deserted** castle. Luckily for us, not even one guard had stayed behind. The Great Discontented One must have felt very secure about where the treasure was **hidden**.

"How do you know where he's hiding it?" Pam asked Nina.

"One day, one of the **RED CAPS** who was guarding us got angry with his companions," Nina explained. "He started moaning and **complaining** and ended up telling me a bunch of things."

"And he told you where the treasure was located?" Colette asked in disbelief.

Nina nodded. "He was convinced that I would never be able to **ESCAPE**."

"Luckily, he was wrong!" Pam commented.

We soon reached a room we had already seen: **the throne room**!

"The treasure is here?" Nicky asked.

Nina pointed under the **tHRONe**. "The Red Cap said it was under there."

"Under the throne?" Colette asked, confused.

"But we'll never be able to move it," Violet pointed out. "It's made of stone, which is **SUPER HEAVY**."

I walked up to the throne and touched it. The stone wasn't cold, and it was **eXTReMeLY** porous. Suddenly, I realized something. It was made of **PUMICE STONE**!

Several months ago, I studied a cave made of pumice stone, and I learned a lot about it. When a stone is porous, it has many **tiny holes** in it, making it weigh less than other stones.

"I think I know how to move the stone," I said.

Everyone stared, waiting for me to explain, but I just placed my hands firmly on the stone and **pushed** hard. The stone easily **SLID** to the side!

"How did you do that, Thea?" Pam asked in disbelief.

I smiled. "It's easy. You try."

Pam placed her paw on it, and the throne easily moved.

"cheese and crackers! THIS Stone is so LiGHt!"

"It must be pumice stone!" Violet concluded brilliantly.

"I should have known," Pam said. "Pumice stone is very LiᵍHᵗ because of the holes all through it, kind of like Swiss cheese."

"And it's the **STONE** used for pedicures," Colette added. "It's an absolute necessity for taking care of your paws."

"It was clever of the Great Discontented One to build a throne that looks heavy but is actually **very light**," Will said. "Well done, Thea, for realizing it!"

"Thanks," I said. "But let's not waste any more time. Let's get the treasure!"

Beneath the throne we found a wooden **trapdoor**, but it didn't have a lock or a handle.

Nicky thought quickly. "This should work," she said, taking a *spear* that was leaning against the wall. She inserted the tip between the floor and the trapdoor and pried it open.

Nicky opened the door all the way, and there was King Waveshaker's treasure, in all its GOLDEN GLORY!

It was so BRIGHt that we had to shield our eyes from the glow. When our eyes adjusted, we realized the treasure was a huge sack of GOLDEN nuggets!

We each grabbed a piece of the sack and

It's the king's treasure!

How beautiful!

hoisted it up from its hiding place. It was much heavier than the throne, but we did it!

"Together we are strong!" Nicky exclaimed.

"Now we can go," Colette said.

"**WAIT!**" I exclaimed.

"What's going on, Thea?" Will asked.

It's opening up!

"I don't think we should leave," I said, and the others looked at me in surprise. "We must stay here and convince the Great Discontented One that he and his people must **never** travel to our world. We've got to make sure that the balance between the two worlds is never disturbed."

"That makes sense," Nicky agreed. "But won't he get really ANGRY when he sees we've got his gold?"

"I'm not going back in a cage," Colette said with a shudder.

Violet looked thoughtful. "I may have an idea," she said. "Follow me!"

We hid the SACK of gold behind a wall in the throne room and then headed back outside, anxious to hear what Violet had in mind.

HAPPINESS IS WHERE YOU LOOK FOR IT

Outside the crumbling castle, the sun was **shining** brightly overhead.

Violet walked to a tree near the river. Its branches were heavy with juicy-looking **FRUIT** as **yellow** as cheese. She picked some and passed it around.

"Aren't these beautiful?" she asked.

"Yes," Pam said, taking a bite. "And **DELICIOUS**, too!"

Violet explained her plan. "I think we should gather everything wonderful that this world offers and show it to the Red Caps. Then maybe they'll see that they can be **happy** right here."

"And that they don't need any treasure," Paulina concluded.

"That sounds like a great **idea**," Nicky agreed. "Well done, Violet."

"Let's each gather whatever we can find," I suggested. "**But hurry!** The Red Caps could return at any moment, and we don't want them to take us by surprise."

It didn't take long to find beautiful things all around us. There were **FLOWERS** with lovely colors and wonderful scents, birds with brightly **COLORED** feathers, and beautiful **INSECTS** and butterflies that looked as though a painter had decorated them.

Will Mystery searched the river. There, he found **seashells** in all different shapes, with smooth surfaces that seemed to **GLITTER**.

I saw COBWEBS on the bushes that looked like fancy **embroidery**, and **beetles** that shone like precious gems.

When each of us had gathered our treasures, we brought them inside the castle. We put everything on the **BIG** table in the throne room and **HID** behind the wall where we had hidden the treasure. Then we waited for the Red Caps to return.

"Are you sure it wouldn't be better to leave while we still can?" Colette asked **nervously**.

"We have to do this," I said. "The Great Discontented One and the Red Caps must understand that they can be **happy** here."

Will and Nina gave me a supportive look. Suddenly, we heard **noises**.

"They're back!" Will cried.

The room filled with Red Caps, who were **eSCORtiNG** the Great Discontented One. They quickly realized that something wasn't right.

"What happened to my **GOLD**?" their leader bellowed when he saw the open trapdoor. "If I find whoever took it, they will feel my **RAGE**!"

I stepped out of my hiding place.

"**It was I**," I said simply.

He stared at me in disbelief. "You? You should be in a **cage**!" he thundered.

Will, Nina, and the Thea Sisters stepped out and stood **BEHIND** me. The Great Discontented One looked as if he might **EXPLODE**. "Guards!" he shouted.

A group of Red Caps stomped toward us, brandishing their **swords**, but I stood firm.

"Can I at least **EXPLAIN** why we took your

gold?" I asked calmly.

"If you must," the leader growled. "But then you're going back in your cage!"

"The gold you **stole** belongs to King Waveshaker," I reminded him. "That is why he's angry, and it's putting the whole Land of Erin in danger."

"**DANGER?** What do you mean?" he asked me, surprised.

Will stepped forward. "I work in a place where we keep track of all of the worlds of fantasy, using special maps. A **large crack** has appeared in the map of the Land of Erin. It's a very serious situation!"

"Waveshaker will **DESTROY** your world if he doesn't get his gold back," Nina added.

The Great Discontented One frowned. "You think I'll just let you take this **TREASURE** from me?"

"It's the only solution," Nina told him.

I **pointed** to the items we had collected on the table. "Look at all of the **WONDERFUL** things that surround you!" I said. "You are so busy complaining that you haven't noticed the **BEAUTY** all around you."

Then Will began to sing a fairy melody, and a **peaceful** feeling descended on everyone in the room.

The Great Discontented One smiled . . . maybe for the **FIRST** time in his life! He looked at the table and exclaimed, "Where did these beautiful things come from?"

How beautiful!

"They are all from this valley, and you can **enjoy**

them every day," Paulina informed him.

Violet smiled. "Now you can see your world —"

"— with fresh **EYES**!" Will finished for her.

The Great Discontented One looked at the table, amazed. "I have never . . ." he murmured, and then his voice trailed off.

"You've never asked yourself why you're so unhappy, have you?" I guessed.

He shook his head slowly, and then a new **SMILE** grew on his face.

"I never have," he said. "Perhaps you are right. It is as though our eyes have been closed all this time. Red Caps, what do you think of all this BEAUTY?"

The **RED CAPS** approached the table, and they slowly began to smile.

"How wonderful!" they cried. They took

in the delicate smell of the colorful FLOWERS. "We really do feel happy!"

I smiled with satisfaction. "I'm so glad. And now we must go."

"You can't stay here with us?" the Great Discontented One asked.

"We must **return** the gold," Colette explained.

"Then we will take you to the court of King Waveshaker!" the Red Caps said.

With that, the Great Discontented One squeezed me and Colette in a big **HUG**!

Thank you! Now I am so happy!

THE COURT OF THE
SPEAKING STONES

I couldn't believe how well things were going. We had found Nina, we were taking the treasure back to King Waveshaker, and we had helped the members of the Court of the Discontented learn to be **happy**.

The Red Caps escorted us through the forest to the Court of the Speaking Stones, where Waveshaker lived. I hoped that the king would **CALM DOWN** once the treasure returned.

Suddenly, the ground beneath our paws rumbled. It was another **earthquake**!

"*That's the king, right?*" Violet asked.

"I think so," I said. "But I'm sure that it will be over soon."

Thankfully, the **tremors** stopped, and no

trees around us fell down. We were safe — for now. The sooner we got to Waveshaker, the better.

I looked behind me. Nina was telling her **STORY** to Will and Pam, who had missed hearing it before.

The Red Caps led us out of the forest into a large field, where we followed a narrow path. I was glad that they were guiding us, because they seemed to know where they were going.

"Hey, what's that up ahead?" Nicky asked, pointing.

The path led to a deep, **rocky gorge**. Our guides carefully led us down into it. They seemed unimpressed, but we were all amazed by the place. Strange faces were carved into the rock walls.

"It's the COURT OF THE SPEAKING

STONES," Nina explained. "Waveshaker lives here. The inhabitants of this place are **ogres**."

Colette's eyes widened.

"OGRES?

THOSE MONSTROUS, ENORMOUSE CREATURES?"

"Yes, those. Yet although they don't look very nice and are very large, they're also very **KIND**," Nina promised.

"That's good news," I replied.

"And we're returning their **TREASURE**," Paulina pointed out, "so they should be **happy** to see us."

I had a feeling that Paulina was right. "Let's go!" I **encouraged** the others. "Our mission is almost complete!"

THE STONE LABYRINTH

We walked through a hole in the rock shaped like a giant mouth. The **paths** of the gorge took us through many **TUNNELS** and passageways. The **rock** walls loomed over us as though they were going to crush us.

After we had walked awhile we heard a voice, deep and echoing, that made us all jump.

"WHY HAVE YOU COME TO THIS PLACE?"

We looked around but couldn't see anyone.

"Who said that?" Nina asked.

"We did!" came the reply.

This time, it sounded like many voices. We realized that the sound was coming from the **STONES**.

"That's why it's called the Court of the **Speaking** Stones," Nicky explained.

One of the **RED CAPS** pointed to a large **cave** in front of us. "The king lives in there," he said.

As we **NEARED** the entrance, a blast of **icy**, moldy air hit us.

"What do you want?" the stones asked us.

"We'd like to see King Waveshaker," I said.

"**Impossible!**" the stones rumbled.

"We have something that belongs to him,

Who said that?

and we'd like to return it," Nina explained.

The stones went quiet for a moment. Then they boomed again.

"ENTER!"

I looked at Nina, uncertain.

"It's all right," she said. "I was here before I was captured. I don't think we're in any **DANGER**. From what I discovered, the Speaking Stones are the **guardians** of Waveshaker's court. They **FRIGHTEN** people with their harsh looks and manners, but once you get to know them, they can be very **kind**."

"Thank you, Nina," I said. "Your research on the Land of Erin has been **EXTREMELY** helpful!"

"I'll be happy to share it with you, once we get back home," Nina said.

"That would be great!" I said. "But first, we have to save this place."

"We will wait for you here," one of the Red Caps said.

We looked at them in surprise.

"Why?" Will asked.

"We stole the king's **TREASURE**. He's **angry** with us," one of them responded.

"But you're returning it to him," Paulina pointed out.

"We'd better not **risk** it. Especially now that we're so HₐPPⱮ," another said, smiling.

"As you wish. **LET'S GO, THEN!**" I said.

We all stepped through the stone doorway together. The inside of the cave was cloaked in **darkness**. When my eyes adjusted, I saw that we were in a corridor of bare stone.

Nina led the way. "These **CAVES** are complex structures, full of corridors that lead to small rooms and narrow passageways."

"IT'S A LABYRINTH!"
Pam realized.

"Yes, all the caves are connected and lead to a central ROOM," Nina explained.

"THE THRONE ROOM!" Colette concluded.

"EXACTLY. And that's where we must go," Nina said. FOLLOWING Nina, we proceeded farther and farther into the maze of corridors.

It's a labyrinth!

KING WAVESHAKER

We walked and walked. **Torches** hanging on the wall of the cave lit our way. The air still smelled fresh, but it got **colder** and **colder** the farther we traveled. From time to time, we could feel the earth below us *trembling*, and it made us nervous. What was waiting for us down there? We would soon find out.

"I think we're almost there," Nina remarked.

We embarked down one last, **STEEP** passageway.

The passage emerged into a large room with a vaulted ceiling. The whole space was entirely carved into the rock. **FLAMING** torches cast a reddish glow on the smooth gray walls.

In the torchlight, we could make out an **ENORMOUSE** creature seated on an **enormouse** throne. In his right hand, he held an **ENORMOUSE** trident. He was the largest creature we had seen in this **LAND**, with **shaggy** hair all over his body.

"Waveshaker," Nina whispered.

The king thumped his trident on the floor, and the whole room began to shake violently.

"That's what's causing the **earthquakes**!" Will whispered excitedly. "The king's anger really is strong enough to **shake** the earth!"

I took a step toward the throne, bowed, and said, "King Waveshaker, we've come from very far away. Our travels have been

full of danger, but nothing could stop us because our goal is to repair every injustice."

The king stared at me with intense black eyes but didn't speak.

"The injustice we are here to remedy is the theft of your GOLD," I continued.

My last word echoed through the cave. *Gold . . . gold . . . gold . . .*

The king stood and thumped his trident on the ground, and the room shook again.

"The treasure of the ogres! My treasure!" he bellowed.

Will understood the seriousness of the situation and quickly pushed the sack of nuggets toward the throne. Waveshaker picked up the sack with his **meaty** hands.

He opened it, and rays of golden light shot from the nuggets, *ILLUMINATING* the entire cave.

"*The treasure of the ogres!*" the king repeated, but this time he sounded happy instead of angry.

The glow dimmed, and we were amazed to see that the nuggets of gold had transformed in the king's hand into a large crown of gold.

The king put it on his head and smiled at us. "Justice is done! Thank you, whoever you are. Thank you! You have brought back the ogres' most precious treasure."

We stared at the crown in **AWE** as the king continued.

"The **crown** has ruled the ogres for a thousand years. I lost my HONOR, and you have restored it to me. I will never forget this!"

Nina was extremely curious. "Your Majesty, can you please explain this **surprising transformation** to us?"

The king thought for a moment, and then he **NODDED**. "By bringing the treasure to me, you have shown yourselves to be faithful friends. I will tell you an ancient **secret** of the ogres," he began. "This crown, which is handed down from father to son, has **magical properties**. When stolen, it turns into gold nuggets so that no one can wear it. This crown can only be worn by the **King of the Ogres**."

"I see," Nina said. "So that is why you were so **ENRAGED** when it was stolen."

"Yes," Waveshaker replied. "If the treasure were mere gold, I would not have been so angry. But this crown is *IMPORTANT* to my people. It is our history."

King Waveshaker set down his trident. "**Peace** will once again reign in the Land of Erin, and in your world, too, you strangers who have come from afar."

The king escorted us back to the entrance of the cave and wished us well. He was so happy that he didn't even ask who had **stolen** his treasure.

AND WE WERE HAPPY TO KEEP THAT SECRET!

OH, no!

We took the long walk back to the surface, where the **RED CAPS** were waiting for us. We told them what had happened, leaving out the secret of the **CROWN**.

The Red Caps **happily** headed back to the Valley of Wishes to tell the Great Discontented One that King Waveshaker was no longer angry. Then we looked to Will's map to find our way **HOME**.

Nina and I had both entered Erin through the **DOOR OF LIGHT** that connected to Ireland, and Will wanted to see it with his own **EYES**. It was a long way off, so we moved quickly.

We were all anxious to return home and present our **amazing** discoveries to the Seven Roses Unit. The Thea Sisters were

enthusiastic, but also a little sad, too. Their mission in the **𝓛𝓪𝓷𝓭 𝓸𝓯 𝓔𝓻𝓲𝓷** had been exciting — much more **EXCITING** than exams at school. They wished they could stay and work with Will and Nina.

"I think you mouselets are ready for a **PROMOTION** at the department," Will said, as though he had read their minds. "I have something special in mind for you. What do you think, Thea? And Nina, would you like to continue **working** with our new friends?"

"Sounds great!" Nina and I both replied.

The THEA SISTERS looked even happier than the Red Caps. They couldn't wait to learn what Will had in store.

"Obviously, though, your work for the **SEVEN ROSES UNIT** must not compromise your **studies** at the academy,"

Will added seriously. "Do you think you'll be able to balance both things?"

"Yes!" the mouselets cried at once, and they hugged us with excitement.

"This is better than a thousand **cheese sandwiches**!" Pam exclaimed happily.

We finally arrived at our destination. The sky was dark, and Nina and I searched for the door. It should have been glowing with light.

"*It should be right here*," Nina murmured, confused, running her hands over a rough, rocky wall.

"Oh, no!" I said, suddenly realizing. "O'Malley must not have been able to keep the FIRE lit, and the passage has closed."

We searched again, but it was clear: There was no trace of the door on the ROCKY wall. The passageway had closed.

"**POOR TeD**," I murmured. "I hope that nothing **BAD** happened to him."

"He's an expert agent," Nina assured me. "He knows how to take care of himself."

"I'm sure he struggled to keep the passage open," Paulina said. "I'll bet he's *worried* about *you*, Thea."

The passage is closed!

"But now what are we going to do?" Colette asked.

"**Simple!**" Will replied. "We'll use the secret portal, which will take all of us to the **HALL OF THE SEVEN ROSES**!"

BACK IN THE REAL WORLD

Will had us stand in a circle and close our eyes. Then he sang a strange MELODY, starting with low tones and building to high tones, and the air around us began to vibrate. When he stopped, we opened our eyes . . . and found ourselves in the crystal elevator!

It **zipped** across the **SPACE-TIME** barrier between the Land of Erin and the real world. It was the first time that I had traveled that way, and I was breathless with excitement.

IT WAS AN EXPERIENCE ON THE EDGE OF REALITY!

Then melodious music swirled around us, and a voice chanted "**SEVEN ROSES**" seven times. The elevator stopped, and we stepped out into the Hall of the Seven Roses.

"How wonderful to be back home!" Nina exclaimed.

I looked around the hall for the maps of the fantasy worlds.

"There's the Land of Erin!" I exclaimed, pointing.

"And the **crack** has disappeared!" Pam cried.

The Thea Sisters came forward to get a closer look, and their eyes shone with **happiness**.

"On behalf of the Seven Roses Unit, I want to express our gratitude to you, Thea, and the THEA SISTERS," Will said. "Without your help, this **mission** would not have

been completed so brilliantly."

The Thea Sisters **BLUSHED**.

"As I've already said, I think you deserve a promotion," Will told them. "What would you say to being **junior researchers** in our department?"

Paulina looked at her friends and responded for all of them.

"OH, WILL, WE WOULD BE HONORED!"

"Great!" Will exclaimed. "This means that you will be able to **HELP** Thea, Nina, and other researchers with their next missions. You'll also be assigned simple projects that you can conduct on your own. Now, remember the code of conduct of the I.I.S.: **Secrecy** is of the utmost importance, as well as **LOYALTY** and **dedication**."

"Of course!" the mouselets replied.

Will grinned. "The I.I.S. is like one **BIG FAMILY**. Our agents are scattered all over the world, ready to lend a paw whenever needed."

I was close to tears. I was so proud of the Thea Sisters!

Nina lightened the mood:

"THIS CALLS FOR A CELEBRATION!"

HOME AT LAST!

"What an exciting trip!" Pam exclaimed as the I.I.S. *speedboat* docked on Whale Island.

"That was a truly incredible adventure," Nicky agreed.

"Yes, but my **fur** is as stringy as mozzarella," Colette complained. "It needs a good conditioning!"

"I'd say that we all need some rest," I remarked. "But first, I want to congratulate you all. I am so proud of you!"

"We did it together," Paulina said.

"Right! We are invincible!" Pam cried, and we all burst out laughing.

As we walked along the dock to the academy, Ruby Flashyfur's huge **YACHT** pulled up to the dock. She hopped off with

her usual air of superiority.

"And where did you DISAPPEAR to?" she asked the Thea Sisters.

Then, looking at me, she added, "Weren't you on a mission with Thea in IReLaND?"

The friends exchanged a surprised LOOK. How did Ruby know about my trip to Ireland?

"What about you, Ruby, were you on **vacation**?" I asked, changing the conversation.

"My exams went so well that my parents sent me on a special trip," Ruby bragged.

"Congratulations, Ruby!" I said. Then I changed my tone. "I'd like to have a chat with your parents, actually. . . ."

"What about?" Ruby asked.

"About your excessive **CURIOSITY** about the conversations of others," I said sternly. "You seem to be very well informed about my mission in Ireland, and I don't remember telling you about it."

She **blushed** with guilt. "Well . . . I . . . I . . ."

I made a point of looking away, and Ruby took the opportunity to leave.

"What a BOTHER she is," Violet said, shaking her head.

"But I'd rather deal with her than a goblin!" Pam joked, and we all laughed.

Then Paulina sighed. "I'd almost rather deal with **goblins** than with another semester of books and tests."

"But you're forgetting one thing," I said.

"What's that?" Paulina asked.

"Well, for one, you never know when Will Mystery may call on you for a **mission**," I reminded them. "And until then, you can have fun with me in my class on investigation under the sea."

The girls all cheered, and then we formed a circle and touched paws.

"HERE'S TO OUR NEXT ADVENTURE — WHATEVER IT MAY BE!"

Don't miss Thea Stilton
and the Thea Sisters' first
special-edition adventure!

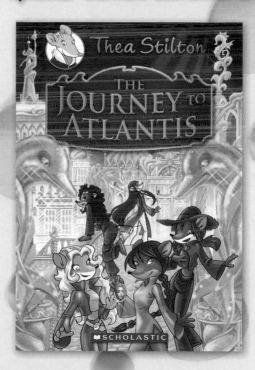

Don't miss any of my fabumouse adventures!

Thea Stilton and the Dragon's Code

Thea Stilton and the Mountain of Fire

Thea Stilton and the Ghost of the Shipwreck

Thea Stilton and the Secret City

Thea Stilton and the Mystery in Paris

Thea Stilton and the Cherry Blossom Adventure

Thea Stilton and the Star Castaways

Thea Stilton: Big Trouble in the Big Apple

Thea Stilton and the Ice Treasure

Thea Stilton and the Secret of the Old Castle

Thea Stilton and the Blue Scarab Hunt

Thea Stilton and the Prince's Emerald

Thea Stilton and the Mystery on the Orient Express

Thea Stilton and the Dancing Shadows

Thea Stilton and the Legend of the Fire Flowers

Thea Stilton and The Spanish Dance Mission

Thea Stilton and The Journey to the Lion's Den

Check out my adventures in the Kingdom of Fantasy!

THE KINGDOM OF FANTASY

THE QUEST FOR PARADISE:
THE RETURN TO THE KINGDOM OF FANTASY

THE AMAZING VOYAGE:
THE THIRD ADVENTURE IN THE KINGDOM OF FANTASY

THE DRAGON PROPHECY:
THE FOURTH ADVENTURE IN THE KINGDOM OF FANTASY

THE VOLCANO OF FIRE:
THE FIFTH ADVENTURE IN THE KINGDOM OF FANTASY

Be sure to read these stories, too!

#1 Lost Treasure of the Emerald Eye

#2 The Curse of the Cheese Pyramid

#3 Cat and Mouse in a Haunted House

#4 I'm Too Fond of My Fur!

#5 Four Mice Deep in the Jungle

#6 Paws Off, Cheddarface!

#7 Red Pizzas for a Blue Count

#8 Attack of the Bandit Cats

#9 A Fabumouse Vacation for Geronimo

#10 All Because of a Cup of Coffee

#11 It's Halloween, You 'Fraidy Mouse!

#12 Merry Christmas, Geronimo!

#13 The Phantom of the Subway

#14 The Temple of the Ruby of Fire

#15 The Mona Mousa Code

#16 A Cheese-Colored Camper

#17 Watch Your Whiskers, Stilton!

#18 Shipwreck on the Pirate Islands

#19 My Name Is Stilton, Geronimo Stilton

#20 Surf's Up, Geronimo!

#21 The Wild, Wild West

#22 The Secret of Cacklefur Castle

A Christmas Tale

#23 Valentine's Day Disaster

#24 Field Trip to Niagara Falls

#25 The Search for Sunken Treasure

#26 The Mummy with No Name

#27 The Christmas Toy Factory

#28 Wedding Crasher

#29 Down and Out Down Under

#30 The Mouse Island Marathon

#31 The Mysterious Cheese Thief

Christmas Catastrophe

#32 Valley of the Giant Skeletons

#33 Geronimo and the Gold Medal Mystery

#34 Geronimo Stilton, Secret Agent

#35 A Very Merry Christmas

#36 Geronimo's Valentine

#37 The Race Across America

#38 A Fabumouse School Adventure

#39 Singing Sensation

#40 The Karate Mouse

#41 Mighty Mount Kilimanjaro

#42 The Peculiar Pumpkin Thief

#43 I'm Not a Supermouse!

#44 The Giant Diamond Robbery

#45 Save the White Whale!

#46 The Haunted Castle

#47 Run for the Hills, Geronimo!

#48 The Mystery in Venice

#49 The Way of the Samurai

#50 This Hotel Is Haunted!

#51 The Enormouse Pearl Heist

#52 Mouse in Space!

#53 Rumble in the Jungle

#54 Get into Gear Stilton

#55 The Golden Statue Plot

#56 Flight of the Red Bandit